WITCH WARRIORS!

"Wherever I may be," Grettir said, "my warriors live here, made from the blood of the crew of your brother. Behold, if you will not come to me, my soldiers will come to you!"

With that, she punctured the red wax covering the opening of the ox horn she held. She inverted the ox horn and shook it at the ground. Bright drops of blood flew forth, and where each struck the ground a Northman warrior sprang up, armed and armored.

Demons who bore the countenances of men Halberd had known since childhood, men whom Halberd had himself buried, now made their way toward him—undead fiends summoned by the witch's hatred to claim Halberd's life!

DREAM QUEST #2

ON THE SHOULDERS OF GIANTS

LLOYD ST. ALCORN

A SIGNET BOOK

NEW AMERICAN LIBRARY

PUBLISHED BY
THE NEW AMERICAN LIBRARY
OF CANADA LIMITED

To
Joy and Jack
&
Danny and Teresa
for everything

NAL BOOKS ARE AVAILABLE AT QUANTITY DISCOUNTS WHEN USED
TO PROMOTE PRODUCTS OR SERVICES. FOR INFORMATION PLEASE
WRITE TO PREMIUM MARKETING DIVISION, NEW AMERICAN LIBRARY,
1633 BROADWAY, NEW YORK, NEW YORK 10019.

First Printing, May, 1988

2 3 4 5 6 7 8 9

SIGNET TRADEMARK REG. U.S. PAT. OFF. AND FOREIGN COUNTRIES
REGISTERED TRADEMARK — MARCA REGISTRADA
HECHO EN WINNIPEG, CANADA

SIGNET, SIGNET CLASSIC, MENTOR, ONYX, PLUME, MERIDIAN
AND NAL BOOKS are published in Canada by The New American
Library of Canada, Limited, 81 Mack Avenue, Scarborough,
Ontario, Canada M1L 1M8
PRINTED IN CANADA
COVER PRINTED IN U.S.A.

Nights of Rain

Halberd was not dreaming. He was trapped in a nightmare, but he could not escape the nightmare by waking. Halberd was not sleeping. He was awake.

Low clouds masked the moon. They had not seen the stars for three nights or the sun for three days. A great storm raged. Howling wind drove the rain sideways. Raindrops smashed the trees like arrows. Bursts of thunder exploded just overhead. The gale-lashed rain drummed into the shields Usuthu wore on his chest and back.

When Halberd looked down below his dangling legs, down below the massive tree branch that he straddled, through the forest of giant trees, he could dimly see the path.

Seeing anything through the storm was difficult. Water poured from the branches above him in a torrent, blocking his eyes and nose. When Halberd held his hand across his forehead he could breathe, almost. The falling rain shot off his hand and formed a small, rushing river before his eyes. He gazed down through this tiny, fierce flow.

The path was barely visible, a narrow, twisting, ill-defined strip of brown mud. The winding brown smear was the only break in the endless forest. The waving branches and thick rain made it seem underwater. The rich green world had become colorless, without any detail. All that remained was the wind, the water, the lightning and the thunder.

But not quite all. Far below, below the madly whipping leaves, below the waving treetop to which Halberd and his men clung, below the blinding bolts of lightning that seemed to strike every tree around them, below the high branches to which they had scrambled in a life-saving panic, stalking through the impassable rain, were the implacable Skrælings.

These Skrælings, members of the tribe called Eerhahkwoi, carried their bows at the ready, one hand on their nocked arrows, one on their bows, with their bowstrings pulled barely taut. Their scout led the way, watching the thick mud and knee-deep puddles for some sign of the Northmen. Though the mud gripped them tightly, ripping the light animal-hide slippers from their feet, the Skrælings did not falter. They moved without apparent effort, appearing more at home in the forest than any other people Halberd had ever seen.

The rain soaked their animal-hide tunics, causing the decorated fabric to stick to their bodies. Their thick black hair, tied into long braids, was tightly plastered to their soaked skulls. The rain had melted the wild paint on their faces into bizarre blocks of indistinguishable color. Beneath this paint their reddish-brown skin gleamed. Halberd could not see their coal-black eyes. The Eerhahkwoi never looked up.

They watched the path ahead and behind, and the tree trunks around them. The Skrælings expected a Northman surprise attack. For good reason. The Eerhahkwoi had learned much about Northman tactics in a short time.

On the huge branch above and to the left of Halberd, sat Usuthu. His broad back rested against the trunk of the giant tree. His long black legs hung free in space. The blurred rain spattered off his conical bronze and leather helmet. Rain ran down his wide, flat cheeks and slanted green eyes. The driving rain boomed off his shields, echoing through Halberd's head as it had for the past three days and nights.

Usuthu did not move. His right hand brushed against his cheek. His left arm was extended in front of him, fully stretched but not locked at the elbow. He held his enormous bow, a huge arrow in place. The bow, which no Viking could string, Usuthu had held at the ready for over half an hour. Ever since the Eerhahkwoi war party had appeared below them. The instant one of the Skrælings looked up, he would die.

That their hiding place would be revealed in such an attack Usuthu cared not. The Mongol giant was tired of hiding. He longed to fight. If he could, he would have dropped to the ground and laid the Skræling party to waste with his curved bronze sword. The eight Skrælings would have proved little match. But the hundreds that would surely follow held Usuthu in check.

A sizzling bolt of lightning flashed through the black sky and struck the tree next to them. The tree caught fire from top to bottom. The giant, pelting raindrops seemed to freeze in midair as the brilliant flames lit everything around them. Looking between his legs, Halberd could see the upturned faces of the Skrælings.

Their mouths fell open as they spotted Usuthu aiming his bow, lit clearly from behind by the flaming tree. One of the Eerhahkwoi raised his arm to point and started to scream. No sound emerged from his mouth before Usuthu's arrow filled it, slamming the Skræling to the soggy earth and pinning him deeply into the mud through the back of his head. The brown splash from the force of his fall rose and broke over his companions like a dirt-filled ocean wave.

The bravest of the Eerhahkwoi raised his bow and let fly at Usuthu. Their arrows passed in the rain-filled night. The Skræling's bolt buried itself into the bark above Halberd's head. Usuthu's took the Skræling full in the chest, snatched him off his feet and hurled him backward through the air. The arrowhead broke through his back and slammed into a tree. The Eerhahkwoi hung from the tree, feet dangling, head lolling in death, blood bubbling from his chest and mixing with the fiendish rain.

Though brave warriors, as their bitter fighting had taught the Northmen, the shocked Skrælings stared in awe at their fallen brother. As Usuthu loosed another arrow the burning tree next to him split with a deafening crack! The flame-filled fracture ran straight to the ground. Broken as if by a giant ax, the two burning halves fell like huge torches through the pelting rain. Usuthu's arrows disappeared to the feathers into one blazing half.

The Skrælings scattered. They could not escape. The two torches dropped through the rain, ripping branches off other trees as they fell. One burning half-tree caught most of the war party as they fled back down the path whence they had come. The tree was easily twenty times the height of a man and as big around as one man is tall. Five Eerhahkwoi vanished under the tree. Their pulped bodies merged with the mud. Bright blood boiled up around the tree as it bounced once and then settled. The splash from its impact marked the surrounding trees with blood and horrible bits of the men who lay beneath it.

Despite the rain and wind, the thunder and lightning, carrion-eating birds appeared and struck at the gore-crusted trunks, pulling off grisly tidbits and vanishing into the night. The remaining Skræling fled the other way, and moved more swiftly than his fellows. He almost survived. The tip end of the other half of the tree smashed against the back of his churning legs. He slammed into the mud, face first.

For a moment he lay still. Then, as the flames licked up his ruined legs and ignited his animal-skin clothes, he began to writhe. He feebly tried to smack the flames out with his hands. But he could not turn over, and his arms slapped at the muddy ground. Too brave and well-disciplined to scream, he pounded his face into the puddles as his flesh seared.

"Usuthu," cried Halberd, "his back is broken. Finish him. Give him a warrior's death."

Usuthu drew back his bow and let fly. The arrow hit the Eerhahkwoi with such force his body flopped off the ground and seemed to curl around the shaft in his back. His head slowly lowered into the mud. A large puddle spread around him, flooding over and covering his head. The puddle was only red for an instant. The nonstop rain quickly washed it brown.

The two tree lengths burned a few minutes more, cracking and snapping in the rain. Slowly they sizzled out, as raindrops spattered into the flames. Soon there was only the sound of the rain and the wind. The blackened trunks covered the path, smoking in the wet night. As the last flickers of flame were extinguished, the mantle of utter darkness fell over the Northmen once more. The booming of the rain off Usuthu's shield did not stop. It never had.

As quickly as the birds had appeared, a great serpent slid from the underbrush surrounding the path. The crack of twigs beneath its weight sounded over the wind and rain. It slid into position in front of the Skræling. The snake's head was larger than the head and back of the Eerhahkwoi. With a ghastly creak the gleaming reptile unhinged his upper jaw and slowly began to work his mouth around the dead Skræling. Halberd turned away. He had seen enough.

The forests in the Unknown World teemed with game as no land he had ever seen. The bottom of the tree in which they hid was marked with the claws of an enormous bear easily the height of two Northmen. Fortunately, the bear had not attempted to scale the tree.

"What was all that disturbance?" a voice shouted into Halberd's ear. Startled, Halberd jumped at the sudden sound, and would have fallen off but for Usuthu's huge hand, which shot through the night and grabbed his shoulder.

Halberd looked above. There, resting comfortably in a hammock strung between two branches, was Mälar, peering through his feet and smiling contentedly. The hammock, made of the skin of a recently slain deer, had not been cured properly. There was no time for such niceties. Accordingly, the hammock stank of rotting flesh. Still, the Northmen could not complain. The deer's raw meat had been their first fresh food in days.

"Mälar," asked Halberd, "have you slept through this storm and the good fortune which slew those who hunted us?"

"That was not good fortune," answered the wily old warrior, "but the deliberate aim of Thor, for it is he who controls the thunderbolts and he also who watches after you."

"If he watches after me so thoroughly, why am I clinging to this branch so that the blood runs from my fingernails and you sleep like a babe?"

"Because he watches after me more closely, young pup, having had much practice through the years. But my old bones are rested now, and if you crave a rest, take this pitiful berth by all means, and dream your dreams in peace."

"Nay, but thanks. The stench of its former occupant would keep me awake no matter how exhausted I may be."

"By that," cried Mälar, "do you mean me or the deer?"

Usuthu, speaking for the first time in the three days and nights since they had raced up the tree like monkeys from the jungles of the Land Where It Is Always Warm, said quietly, "Take your rest, my brother. Perhaps your dreams will grant us the path through this World. Awake, we have solved none of our problems."

Halberd looked down. There, curled like a babe in the crotch of three twining branches, slept his older brother, Labrans. Since well before their arrival on the shore of the Unknown World, Labrans had been enslaved by the witchcraft of Grettir, the human demon whom they had pursued to the Unknown World and who now turned all the Skrælings against them.

Her spell, powerful when they were leagues away, was overwhelming now that they trod upon the earth of the Unknown World. Since they had waded ashore, Labrans had not spoken, except in response to the witch's commands. His eyes were dull and glazed, his limbs slack and his reflexes slow.

Halberd, certain that Grettir watched them through

the eyes and ears of his possessed brother, waited in fear of the moment when Labrans, on the witch's orders, would raise his sword and try to kill one of them. Then Halberd would have to strike against his own blood. Halberd dreaded that moment with all his heart.

"Sleep, Halberd," Mälar said gently. "We will watch him closely. If he tries to flee, we will bind him. If he tries to kill us, we will prevent it."

"Prevent it with care," Halberd replied. "Beneath that hideous spell beats the heart of my brother. Though it would break my heart, I can kill him, if I must. I could not bear, nor would I allow either of you to do it for me. Only shared blood may spill shared blood."

"Then spill it now!" Mälar blurted as he swung from his hammock and onto the huge branch beside Halberd. "Do not wait until you are vulnerable. Slay him before he lashes out upon the witch's command yet again. In your heart you long for some cure of this enchantment, but in your head you know the truth! Labrans will not be saved. If you let him live you imperil the rest of us."

Usuthu turned his back to the conversation and rested his head against the tree trunk. He closed his green-yellow slanted eyes. Years of hard riding on the Great Steppes had taught him to sleep in the saddle, even in a hailstorm. A sopping tree in a driving rain was a softer bed than that. As for the argument, Usuthu possessed no doubt as to its outcome. Mälar and Halberd had had it often before. Usuthu was asleep in an instant.

13

"Could you really do, it old man?" asked Halberd. "Could you put the knife in your own brother while he slept, helpless, caught in the web of a spell?"

"My brothers are all long dead," Mälar spat, the rain coursing off his bony forehead, his eyes bright, "except for Allain, and he spends so much time praying he might as well be. The question is not whether I could sink a knife into my brother, but if I could sink one into yours. The answer to that question is yes."

Halberd seized the old man's wiry forearm and squeezed until his knuckles went white.

"Do not speak of my family in this way, Mälar," he whispered ferociously, restraining himself with great effort. "I will slit my throat before I harm you, as you well know. My heart cannot bear to hear my brother's death called for so eagerly. My emotions will rule me and I cannot bear the consequences. Even more than on our ocean journey we must hold together as a crew."

Another jagged bolt split the sky and thunder crashed about them. The rain blew even harder.

"If we are a crew," Mälar whispered into his ear, "then you must act as our captain. No sacrifice is too great for the good of all. Be cautioned by the Death of Jarl."

Despite the dire nature of their talk, despite the necessity of whispering into the teeth of the gale lest Grettir's sleeping servant Labrans overhear, Halberd burst into laughter.

"Jarl," he gasped. "You would throw that child's

tale in my face at this hour, in this storm, old man? Aye, you are ruthless. That tale is old enough to grow hair, and a full gray beard besides. Speak to me not of the Lost Eons."

"The Death of Jarl is not so old or so false as you imply. I saw Jarl's death with these eyes on my second voyage to the Land of Sand on the Inland Sea. I saw it. I was there."

Mälar looked off, through the wind and the waving trees, toward the east, back toward the Land of Sand uncountable leagues distant. Mälar was old, but he seldom discussed his youth. He was not a teller of tales. He lived his life to the fullest. Mälar had not yet settled his old bones by the fire, the better to relive his life in song and story. He intended to die on an adventure. He seldom indulged in the sentimentality of nostalgia. But now he was lost in a memory of great power.

"The voyage was smooth and uneventful," he began. "We swapped a dragon-ship of booty taken without loss of life from the monks of Lyndisfarne to the slave traders whose skin is the same color as Usuthu's. Much silver did we load and fine weapons besides. This very dagger . . ."

The old sea dog slid one hand beneath his wringing tunic and produced a slender, vicious blade. The silver handle, once deeply etched with carved scenes, was worn smooth by decades of handling.

". . . was my personal prize. The voyage back was miserable. Once past the Guardian Rock we hit fierce storms. Our crew was decent enough, neither great sailors nor poor ones, though their luck was pitiful. Of course, as a stupid young man, I thought that they were gods. For many days we ate no fresh food, only dried meat and casked water. We blew into unknown seas and fought serpents. We struggled without wind for days and without stars for many nights. We were lost.

"After perhaps three weeks, Jarl, our foreman, awoke with the Disease of Bleeding Gums. We saw the spatters of his blood floating on the surface of the water in the cask. He looked at the blood and we all stared at him in silence. Jarl was a big man and a fine warrior. No one wanted to tell him the bad news. Yet he did not require our advice. He raised one hand to his gums to confirm the awful truth, and that hand came away damp and red."

Mälar leaned closer to Halberd as the wind tried to fling them from the tree. The stinging raindrops bounced off Mälar's cheek, but his teeth and eyes shone in the blackness. His face almost touched Halberd's.

"He stood straight and tall, as a Northman should. He fastened on his sword and his shield and slid his fighting mace into its holster. His bag of silver he threw upon the deck for all to share, and he strode to the gunwale.

"The warriors aboard knew what to expect. What did I know? Nothing! I was an ignorant child, I knew ought of the sea, but even I knew this: If a man appears with the Bleeding Gums, then no man will survive the journey. First one man has it, then the next and the next until all are dead and the ship drifts at sea, flesh rotting on the deck and no hand to guide the tiller. Even I knew that."

Mälar paused for a breath. Halberd stared into the rain, seeing the ship in his mind as Mälar described it, all frozen in fear, all watching Jarl, only a few old salts anticipating what would follow.

"Jarl went to the gunwale and turned to the rest of us. 'Remember me!' he shouted. 'Tell my family I died like a man. I take my weapons so that I may fight you when we meet again in Aasgard.'

"He flung himself into the sea and began to swim away. He turned on his back and spouted water like the Great Fish Who Suckle Their Young, the Fish of Oil. He swam on his back until the waves blocked him from our view.

"That is the Northman way. He gave himself to save the ship. He made the sacrifice. If he had not, we would have flung him over the side. If he had stayed aboard all would have died. Worse, if we had killed him then many blood feuds would have begun. It would have meant virtually a war between the crew and our own village. It was intolerable! There was no solution until Jarl made the impossible choice.

"And now you must do the same, only your task is more difficult than Jarl's. It is easy to give one's own life to heroism, but impossible to take another's for the same purpose. Yet this you must do.

"If I slay him, or if Usuthu wields the knife, I fear the spell will leave Labrans and seize us. Only you may do the deed without fear. Believe me, Halberd, Labrans is a dead man who still walks.

17

While he walks we must fear him. When he is a dead man who cannot walk, then are we safe.

"I have had my say. I'll speak of it no more."

Halberd thought for many minutes. His hand rested lightly on the blade of his battle-ax. To slay his sleeping brother would be simple. There was no doubt that his brother was enslaved, no doubt that Labrans wished them only harm.

But there was one all-important doubt.

"Old man," Halberd began, his heart filled with love for the courage required for Mälar to speak so plainly. "As a shaman I have much to learn, but still I have learned much already. I have seen things other men may not see and I possess objects of unearthly power that other men may not possess. I slew Fallat when all claimed he was invincible and I slew the dwarf, Thund, though no other man that we have ever heard of has slain an Immortal.

"The world of magic is my true home and yet there is only one thing I know with certainty. And that is that there is no certainty. Not in the land of magic. Any spell may be broken, any demon may be bested and any immortal may be slain. Despite Grettir's powers, and she is the strongest witch either of us has ever seen, we must not believe that she is unbeatable. Her spell may one day free Labrans, or he may free himself from it. Until the day he again raises a weapon against me or my crew I must remain his brother and so I shall."

Mälar said nothing. The rain pounded against the tree trunk and the wind howled in their ears.

Halberd breathed easily, his choice made, his course, at least in this matter, clear.

"You are my captain," said Mälar. "I went on this mad voyage for adventure and you have given me my fill of it. I may die hungry in this Unknown World, or frightened, or run through by the lances of savages so uncivilized they still use stones for their arrowheads. One thing I know: I will not die bored and this is more than most men can say, even most Northmen.

"This is your decision. It is sentimental and foolish and will bring you harm. It may even bring me harm, but I will not question it. When I was young and stupid, I, too, was sentimental. But if I accept this course, you must swear to me that the moment Labrans strikes at you I am free to whack off his head. That I am free to pursue my instincts and take from the witch Grettir her servant."

"This I swear," said Halberd.

"Then sleep, Shaman. Perhaps a solution lies in your dreams."

Halberd climbed gingerly over the old seaman and straddled the branches from which the hammock was hung. The deerskin reeked of meat. Small crunchy insects roamed inside it, munching noisily on the flesh still clinging to it. Still, it was almost a bed. Halberd unclasped his armor and hung it on a small nubbin. His shoulder scabbard holding his broadsword he unstrapped and lay across him, one hand on the inlaid handle, the Jewel of Kyrwyn-Coyne nestling in its spider-web filigree of silver at the butt of the sword.

He squirmed about in the hammock. Crushing the insects with his back, he made the deerskin as comfortable as he could. He draped his face with a piece of his cloak, and for once the rain no longer pounded on it.

He would sleep shortly, but he had much to think about.

He thought of how they had come to the Unknown World.

The Shore of the Unknown World

Halberd nestled deeper in the hammock. He was so glad to be lying down, he scarcely noticed the smell. It had been many days since they had rested. And what poor quality of rest this nest afforded—the hammock was soft, but the rain never let up and the wind blew him about like a sail. And it was cold, not so cold as Northland in winter, and certainly nothing like Vinland, but still cold.

Why did the rain and wind make him so restless? Usuthu slept without noticing. Mälar never stirred. Halberd knew he had been through longer, colder spells than this on board ship, fighting fierce storms and praying that the waves wouldn't swamp his craft.

"Mälar," he called over the wind, "why does this storm vex me so? I've fought much worse than this, while clinging to a lifeline just to stay alive. Here my life is in no immediate jeopardy, yet I can't bear another drop striking me."

"Because now you are bored," came the reply. "When you fight for your life you're distracted from the weather. When waiting is your only task, time slows until waiting is intolerable. Warriors can do many things, especially young warriors, but waiting is not one of them."

"Aye, but what are we waiting for?" Now that he was physically relaxed for the first time in days, Halberd's spirits sank.

"Be full of strength, Halberd. We are waiting for this cursed storm to lift so that we may climb down from this tree and move through this impenetrable forest so that we may find the trail of the witch Grettir so that you may cut out her heart and serve each of us a generous slice.

"And," the tough old man continued, "while we search for her she works her magic among the Skrælings so that none will give us shelter or aid and all look to kill us as we travel."

"I wonder," said Halberd, "when other warriors from the village of these dead ones will come looking for their companions."

"Given what we've seen, I don't think any will emerge until the storm abates. By then, I trust, we shall be long gone."

"Aye, at first light, regardless of weather and even of serpents the size of dragon-ships, we must be off."

"Where shall we go, young shaman?"

"To the Great Falls that Ishlanawanda says lies to the northwest. There are several mountain ranges between us and the falls, but if it is the place of power the savages claim, then Grettir should be camped nearby."

"What say your dreams on this matter?"

"Little. Since our first night I cannot reach the village of my dream guide. Without her I can make but little sense of our plight. But Grettir knows we are nigh. She cannot help but show herself to us. She will guide us to her lair, intentionally or not."

"Talk no more. Sleep now. You will not sleep on your back for several nights to come, I fear."

Mälar turned his gaze into the wind and drew his cloak about his face.

Halberd tried to sleep, but his mind was full of the path that led them to this tall tree in this driving storm. . . .

They had bobbed offshore in their Skræling skin canoe. Labrans sat wordlessly in the bow, Usuthu behind him, Halberd behind the black Mongol giant and Mälar, the navigator and helmsman, ruled the stern.

Before them lay the Unknown World. They were the first of their kind, excepting Grettir, to venture this far to the west. There were no legends to guide them, no charts, no tales told by old salts at the fire in the stone great-houses. Soon they would step on Terra Incognita, the Unknown World. What gods ruled there, what beasts walked, what men lived and died they knew not. They only knew that Grettir waited.

Grettir had come to Vinland, the vast ice-choked isle that lay halfway between Northland and the Unknown World, with Halberd's eldest brother, Valdane. With an able crew they had arrived to

23

establish a settlement, perhaps a base from which to explore the Unknown World.

In the course of their time on Vinland, Grettir had changed. She consorted with the Skræling host there, learned their language and their spells and had called upon the darkest forces in Niflheim, the Underworld Land of the Dead. Grettir became a potent Skræling witch. With the aid of two fiendish Dwarfs from the Underworld, she slew Valdane and all his crew and fled to the Unknown World. Visiting Halberd in a dream, she showed him the murder of his brother and challenged him to follow her for his revenge.

Halberd had little choice. Grettir was not only Valdane's wife, she was also Halberd's secret lover. On the day of her marriage to Valdane, Grettir had come to Halberd and they had consummated their unspoken love. Deep in his soul, Halberd feared that his treachery had loosened the demons in Grettir's heart.

Soon Halberd had a ship and a crew. They sailed to Vinland, fought the Skrælings and learned much from the ghost of one of his brother's crew and, ultimately, from the doomed ghost of Valdane himself.

On Vinland Halberd slew the fearsome dwarf, Thund, using the same odd stone knife with which Grettir killed Valdane. No mortal had ever slain an Immortal before and no one knew what the consequences might be. When Thund died, six months of winter passed in one day, and Vinland was inundated with floods from the melting ice and snow.

Halberd's surviving crew, less the three who now slept in the branches, steered their dragon-ship northeast, back to Northland.

Halberd, Labrans, Usuthu and Mälar sailed southwest in their skin canoe, searching for the Unknown World.

On Vinland, via the Dream World through which Halberd could travel as no other shaman, Halberd found something equal to all his knowledge: he found love. Living in a peaceful village in the Dream World was the Skræling woman, Ishlanawanda. She repeatedly sought Halberd out as he sailed west, and as he departed Vinland, she took him to the edge of her village.

When he finally arrived in the Unknown World, she promised, they would be able to touch. But for a brief visit when he sought landfall, he could not find her village, though he traveled through the Dream World as far as he dared. Her village was lost to him.

Halberd suspected some treachery of Grettir's lay at the heart of this mystery, but he knew only Ishlanawanda or the witch herself could show him the way.

A new gust of wind blew his hammock hard against the tree. Halberd's shoulder whacked the trunk. He tried to sleep once more, but sleep would not come. So Halberd sought to lose himself in thoughts of their journey to this miserable, soaking roost . . .

*   *   *

After sailing through fog, relying on ocean currents and the will of the Norns to guide them, they had reached the Unknown World.

From north to south, as far as they could see, lay a ghostly coastline. Shrouded in trees to the water's edge, the coast was low and appeared fairly flat. No great mountains or fjords split its walls; no high peaks appeared in the distance. No huge waves crashed on the shore. The trees were deep green and undulated softly in the wind. There was no beach.

Halberd gazed at the coastline with powerfully mixed emotions. He had sailed farther than any man in the Known World, their journey had surpassed legend, and adventures unimaginable awaited them ashore. Yet his heart was heavy. He had not sailed this far for glory or for exploration, but only revenge. However his spirit might rise at the thought of their accomplishment, it sank when he thought of what lay ahead. Joy would elude him, he knew, until he held Grettir's head in his hands and his brother's ghost no longer dwelled in the icy depths of Niflheim.

Halberd found he could not speak. His emotions had taken hold of him. He turned slightly and nodded to Mälar.

"Well," said Mälar, breaking the reverent silence, "we are explorers and that is undoubtedly land. Shall we not make for it?"

"Aye," said Usuthu, who deeply feared the sea, "let us tread where nothing moves beneath our feet. Let us drink from a spring and not a skin,

and eat meat which lived moments before it became our supper, instead of weeks."

"Forward, then," said Halberd, and all bent their
paddles to the gentle sea.

The canoe cut across the smooth water, rocking
slightly with the wind-driven chop. Labrans stared
apathetically ahead, his paddle resting across his
lap. The nearer they drew to the Unknown World,
the less he spoke or ate or drank. Since Halberd
could not see over or around Usuthu's huge back,
he paddled looking down.

When they were within two boat-lengths of the
shore Halberd heard a tiny splash beside the boat. He
raised his head expectantly, looking for a sea otter
or seal or some playful beast of the shallow sea.
Instead the splash was repeated. Was it raining?
He looked to the low gray sky.

"Back!" called Usuthu, an arrow protruding from
the skin of the canoe by his side. "We are attacked!"

The gentle splash became a hail of arrows. Halberd and Mälar swung their shields from the sides
of the canoe and held them overhead. Stone arrowheads clanged off the hide and bronze shields.

Usuthu dug his paddle into the sea and back-
stroked with all his might. The bow of the canoe
pulled down into the sea, soaking Labrans. He said
nothing. Another stroke with the opposite blade of
Usuthu's double-ended paddle, and the canoe shot
backwards. Another cluster of arrows hit the water
just in front of the canoe. Then they were out of
range.

High ululating screams filled the air. Still, no

human was visible. The arrows emerged from the trees.

"Turn to," said Mälar. "I want a shot at these beasts."

He hefted his bow. Usuthu had already pulled his up and ready. An arrow was in the string. His paddle rested across the canoe. Halberd looked around the canoe and pulled arrows from the sides and the top, searching to see if any of their fresh-water skins had been punctured. All appeared safe. The arrows were much like those used by the Skrælings on Vinland: long shafts painted in bright colors, razor-sharp stone arrowheads and small tufts of bird feathers at the tail.

The three men were panting from surprise and exertion. Mälar and Usuthu held their bows at the ready, waiting for a target to appear. Halberd, using his paddle deftly, turned their boat sideways to the shore, providing a clean shot at whoever might emerge.

Their canoe was based on Skræling design. It was not a long, open boat but a narrow craft, completely covered with sea-mammal hide, with openings only large enough for each man to sit in. A watertight skirt of hide encircled their waists and they sat on the bottom of the boat. Their legs stretched in front of them beneath the skin top of the canoe. They were exposed only from the waist up. Their gear was hung from the outside. It was a stable, dry craft, safe in high water, good in smooth seas and an excellent platform from which to shoot.

Shouting erupted from the woods and at least

twenty Skrælings burst from the trees and raced into the shallow water. Halberd back-paddled the canoe a bit more.

"Hold fire," said Mälar. "This is a curious sight. These are like no men I've ever seen, if indeed they are men. Don't drive them away."

"We are out of range," said Usuthu. "They cannot harm us."

The Skrælings stopped their charge some distance from the canoe. They stood in waist-deep water and shook their weapons and fists at the Northmen.

These Skrælings were taller than those on Vinland, and less squat in build, with broad chests and shoulders. Their skin was an odd reddish-brown, gleaming with bright paint on their cheeks and hands. Their eyes were slanted and deep black. Their hair was shiny black and very long, hung in braids or flowing free. The hair at the center of their heads stood up in a long, thin line that ran from the forehead to the back of the neck. They wore feathers in their hair, and necklaces of large animal claws.

Their clothing was also startling. They wore fringed animal-skin leggings and colored cloths flapped free at the top of the leggings, covering their groins. Their tunics were animal-hide and brightly decorated. They bore war clubs with huge stones attached to stout branches by hide wrappings. Their bows were simple and they carried no shields. A few brandished lances with stone heads.

They shook their fists and clubs at the Northmen

and shouted in their incomprehensible tongue. They made no move to draw closer.

"Usuthu, the Skrælings of this tribe resemble you," said Halberd.

"Yes," the giant replied, "their skin is a different hue, but their eyes and their shape suggest they could be the larger cousins to my clan. Have we sailed so far west we have come to the Farthest East? Are we near the land of the Great Khan?"

"I think not," said Mälar. "We could not have circled the Earth in our short time at sea."

"They will not attack us. If that was their aim they could come nearer still," said Halberd. "They seek to drive us away."

"Yes." Usuthu nodded his head as he spoke, one eye on the Skrælings. "They fear us, as did the demons on Vinland. There are no women in this group. It is a war party sent to protect a village."

"Can Grettir have turned the inhabitants of this world against us already?" asked Mälar. "Truly her power is great. I had hoped for some native allies in this land. If we three fight alone, our task is prodigious indeed."

"Four, Mälar, not three," said Halberd. He nodded toward his brother in the bow. Labrans ignored them.

Labrans watched the Skrælings from beneath lowered brows. His shoulders slumped forward and none behind him could see his face. Labrans smiled a soft, secret smile.

"However many our noble force may be," said Mälar, "we cannot land here."

They stowed their weapons once again and back-paddled another half league from land. The Skrælings watched with uncertainty, their weapons at their sides, their faces slack. Perhaps they wanted a fight, after all. When the Northman canoe turned toward the south and began to move away, the Skrælings stayed a moment longer and then straggled back into the woods. The coastline was quiet again.

The Northmen said nothing. They knew their duty. They paddled south and west, following the curve of the land. The coast grew rocky, broken with boiling currents trapped between jutting pillars of rock. The trees receded, leaving high, fat rocks and bare cliffs rising from the sea.

"Behold," called Usuthu.

Mälar and Halberd gazed down the path of his outstretched arm. Resting by a fire on one windy rock was a Skræling scout. When he saw the canoe he stood, silhouetted by the afternoon sun. He shook his lance at the Northmen threateningly and then gestured to the west with a wide sweep of his arm.

"At last they send us a clear message: If you want to live, keep moving," said Mälar.

"Aye," said Halberd. "It pleases them for us to sail westward. But is it their fear or Grettir's hand which offers this advice? Does a trap await us? Are we sailing into some dragon's lair?"

"We shall not know until it happens," answered Mälar. "They don't want us to land, and there are more of them than there are of us. Could the situation be any simpler?"

"No," said Usuthu shortly. He dug his paddle into the sea.

By nightfall they had passed more such outposts than they could count. Every Skræling had waved them on. In the coves with shallow, accessible beaches, war parties stood guard. The coastline was a fortress, ready to repulse any attack.

As the sun's chariot pulled it across the sky and into darkness, another surprise awaited. The coastline abruptly ended. The coast they had followed curved back to the Northeast. They were once again in open sea.

"Is that all there is of the Unknown World? Are we again in the Great Open Ocean?" Usuthu asked.

"No, you landlocked savage," said Mälar. "We circled across the southern end of a great island or penninsula. Across this sea we shall find the land mass of the Unknown World."

"One day I hope you awake on the Great Steppes," said the Mongol, "surrounded by yellow hills for a thousand leagues in all directions, with no tree or brook or even a stone to mark your path. Then we shall see how certain you are."

"Should this occur," replied Mälar, "I trust that I shall have you by my side, to guide me through that world which you know so well, just as you have me by your side today for that very same purpose."

"How can you speak with such surety? You do not recognize the stars in this western sky."

"Look around you, man! Gulls fill the sky to the

west, and so do land-based birds of prey. We have only a short journey yet."

"Another night on this water," said Usuthu, "will not seem short to me."

Their Skræling canoe was a worthy craft, but it was still a canoe, not a dragon-ship. They could not lie down, move about or even stand. They had defeated dragons in the Great Open Ocean, but they had fought from the broad decks of the *Freyja*. A dragon attack here might end differently. If Hel decided to seek revenge for the death of her servant, Thund, she might dispatch the Great Serpent, Niddhogg himself. If Niddhogg swam up from the Underworld, they were doomed.

Again they drifted with the westward current and again morning brought landfall. This coast was different, foreboding, almost desolate. The rocky shoreline showed no easy landing places. There were few trees near the waterline and little cover. The coast was broken into hundreds of little inlets and harbors, all shrouded by high surrounding hills and cut off from the sea by swirling currents.

As they chewed their morning ration of dried meat and swigged stale water from a skin, Halberd spoke with finality. "We must land," he said. "I cannot bear another night. I have felt no blood run through my legs nor that which I sit upon in three days. Find the nearest calm harbor and let us make a camp."

They paddled cautiously into a small beach which lay tucked inside two large horns of land. As the water went from black to clear Halberd at last saw bottom. He braced his hands on the sides of the canoe, lifting himself and stretching his watertight skirt. He reached down to open the ties that bound him in.

A rough blow struck his chest. He was hurled backward into his seat by an unseen hand. A loud thump filled his ears. Protruding from his chest armor was a Skræling arrow. It had not penetrated to his flesh. The Skrælings had triggered their ambush too soon. They were not within killing range.

The hills echoed with a high, wavering cry. Another war party, clad as the first, boiled out of the woods. The surrounding horns of land were lined with Skræling warriors. Their arrows filled the sky. Most fell short. The Skrælings would not come near enough to the shore to engage in a real fight. They sought only to drive the Vikings away. The weary Northmen back-paddled in disgust.

They drifted down the broken shoreline all day, goaded by Skræling patrols.

"How can these demons send messages over such distances?" asked Mälar. "Does Ishlanawanda speak to them in their dreams?"

"Tomorrow we shall make land," said Halberd, his rump aching. "Prepare your weapons, for we will not retreat again."

That night brought howling rains and fierce winds. Mälar made a sea anchor of his cloak and they rode out in the storm in misery.

Near dawn, as the gray sky lightened and the rain lessened slightly, Halberd awoke to a stirring at the bow. Labrans sat upright. After glancing furtively at Usuthu, who rode right behind him, Labrans laid his paddle, which he had not wielded in days, gently into the swelling sea. It floated quickly out of his reach. Halberd struggled from his exhausting half-sleep. He tried to decipher his brother's actions. Had the witch's spell been lifted? Or was it just now being put into action? Usuthu's enormous slumping back prevented Halberd from seeing Labrans clearly.

Labrans' hand appeared near the gunwale. Stealthily the bewitched Northman drew his broadsword from its scabbard, which hung on the side of the canoe. Halberd watched with his breath caught, torn between the fear that Labrans might wield his sword against Usuthu and the desire to discover his brother's purpose.

Labrans lay the sword across his lap. Halberd could not see his next action, but he heard a swift cutting sound, as if Labrans was rending the hide skirt which secured him to the canoe.

At that instant there was no more stealth. Labrans, showing a balance he had lacked prior to enchantment, pushed against the gunwales of the canoe and came to his feet like a cat, balancing in the narrow craft despite the rocking sea. It was not human.

Labrans raised the sword above his head, gripping with two hands. Rain splashed off the gleaming blade, A crack of lightning split the sky and showed his clenched teeth and mad eyes. Thunder boomed. The night went black once more. Usuthu and Mälar raised their nodding heads.

"No, my brother!" screamed Halberd. "Deny the witch! Fight her for memory of our dead brother, Valdane!"

Halberd grabbed for his own sword, certain he had sacrificed Usuthu's life by his fumbling. The Jewel of Krywyn-Coyne at the butt of his sword glowed like fire. The jewel lit up only when a dream-prophesy was true or the power of the spirit world was near. At this awful moment its light burned through the increasing rain.

The dark force of Grettir's magic was all around them.

Usuthu came instantly awake and reached for Labrans' leg.

As the Mongol's fingers closed on his calf, Labrans swung his iron sword.

"Oh, my beloved mistress," Labrans shrieked like a demon, "now is the time!"

With one wide swing of his razor-sharp blade, Labrans cut the entire front off the canoe. His sword tore through the skin and wooden frame just as Usuthu snatched him backward. Labrans lurched and, twisting against the giant's grip, yanked the canoe sideways. Labrans was pitched into the sea.

The nose of the canoe filled with water even as it capsized, flipping Halberd, Mälar and Usuthu. Halberd slashed the hide skirt with his dagger, clinging to his broadsword with the other hand. If he could not free the skirt he would die upside-down. One man might roll such a canoe, but not three.

As he chopped, Halberd had but one thought: Usuthu could not swim! He must be rescued. The skirt opened and Halberd slid into the dark sea. He kicked free of the canoe and pushed for the surface. His leather armor and weapons pulled him down, but he kicked harder. His head broke through the iron-gray swells. He opened his mouth to breathe and a wave broke across his face.

Coughing and spitting, pulling at his chest armor and feeling into the pockets sewn across its back, Halberd confirmed that Hrungnir, the pyramid-shaped stone knife, still rested snug in its hidden holster. He slid his broadsword back into its shoulder scabbard and clasped the silver handle with a small hide loop hung there for that purpose. Halberd trod water with one hand while he held his dagger above the surface. He saw no one else.

He took a deep breath and dove beneath the waves. Usuthu was trapped upside-down in the canoe. He was pulling against the hide skirt with all his strength. Halberd gripped the side of the canoe and carefully cut the hide. Usuthu sat perfectly still. He crossed his arms over his chest. The slashed hide released the Mongol. He thrashed himself clear of the canoe and rose to the air.

Their heads above water, Halberd reached for Usuthu and guided them onto his back.

"Lay there and be still," Halberd called. "Spread your arms wide. You will not sink."

Usuthu did as he was bade. His bow was in one hand, his great quiver in the other. The magical silver hammer rode about his neck, tied to a thong.

"Did Mälar free himself? The sea is too dark to tell."

"I do not know, my brother," Usuthu gasped. He would not raise his head from the surface.

"I must find him. Float quietly. If you see Labrans, just kick away from him. He is in the witch's spell and that spell is now unleashed."

"This," the Mongol said softly, "I know."

Halberd dove under the overturned craft again. It was filled with water and pointed straight down. It could sink at any moment. Only its stern still floated on the surface. Halberd groped his way down the canoe and found, with his hands, Mälar pulling at the side of the craft. When Halberd touched him, Mälar swung blindly. Halberd grabbed him and yanked him to the top of the rolling waves.

"It is I, you old fool! What are you doing down there?"

"All our water and weapons will be lost," Mälar gasped and sputtered. "We must go back and retrieve the bags."

"Have you seen Labrans?"

"No. Here, give me your dagger and tend to the Mongol. We've no time. No time!"

Halberd handed over his slender blade and Mälar disappeared. Halberd, treading water and craning his head over the waves, saw Usuthu drifting away. He swam quickly to the giant and took him by the feet. Halberd gently towed Usuthu toward the canoe.

"Patience," Halberd called, "I will not let you drown."

"Nor I you," he answered.

Halberd pulled Usuthu to the stern of the canoe. Though he felt the weight of his weapons and armor, Halberd, like all his village, had learned to swim before he could walk. He was strong.

It felt good to be free after the long days of confinement in the canoe. It was right and just to be struggling in the waves and wind, death all around. This was a Viking's lot. As Halberd reached the stern a skin of water bobbed to the surface. He grabbed it and swung Usuthu around.

"Clasp this like your sweetheart, if ever you had one, and do not let go."

"What of the serpents of the sea?" Usuthu asked as he wrapped his huge arms around the bulging skin.

"I do not think they come this near to shore," Halberd lied. He had thought of the serpents, too. "Beware instead of Labrans. He swims as well as any serpent. If other skins rise near you, seize them, too."

Halberd did not see Usuthu's nod of assent. He hoped the lie had calmed his friend. The Viking dove again and passed Mälar as the old sailor made for the surface, his arms laden with weapons. Halberd ran his hands down the sides of the canoe. As soon as he extended his arm he lost sight of his hands. The blackness of the sea, even at this depth, was complete. Halberd forced himself deeper, tearing each bag of provisions still attached to the craft. He cursed himself for not taking his dagger back from Mälar.

Halberd reached the truncated bow and started back up again. His lungs burned for air. The canoe lurched perfectly upright and raced through his hands, heading for the bottom like a lance. Halberd could not believe the speed with which the rough skin passed across his hands. The canoe fell away and Halberd swam upward.

As he did, rough hands seized his waist and yanked down. Without thought Halberd kicked downward, aiming where the shoulders might be. He connected perfectly, feeling the head snap back. With his last ounce of reserve Halberd reached down and took his poor, accursed, unconscious brother by the hair. He kicked for the surface with all his might.

He broke into a raging storm. The waves whipped across his face, broken at the top with whitecaps. The wind sang in his ears and in it, woven through it, Halberd could hear the laughter of Grettir.

"Swim, my love," she cried into the night, her voice mixed with the wind. The hair rose on the back of his neck. "Don't die in this awful sea. Swim to my lips, my arms, my legs. Swim to me, to my embrace."

Halberd tucked the sleeping head of his brother under his arm and swam easily through the swells, towing Labrans behind him. He twisted his head for Mälar and called his name into the wind.

Halberd slid down the lee side of a wave and found, in its trough, Mälar and Usuthu rapidly lashing a rough raft, tieing all the water skins together with hide wrappings, and then securing the weapons, blankets and furs they had salvaged to the bundle of skins.

The skins formed a ragged circle, atop which

rode Mälar's leather armor, sword and ax, two sleeping furs and a few blankets. Strips of dried fish and meat hung from the skins. Usuthu bobbed in the center of this rough circle, clinging to the skins and fighting down his terror at the only thing on Earth that he feared: the sea.

"Where is the dawn?" Halberd called.

Mälar replied, "Grettir holds this storm over our heads. She will keep it in place until we are drowned. I do not think the sun will rise in this place before then."

"Can you remember which way toward land?" Halberd screamed into the old man's ear in order to be heard over the wind.

"I must have a bearing to find my way," he answered. "Without the sun or stars all we can do is float."

"Can you not hear the witch in the wind?"

"No, I hear only my heart beating," said Mälar.

"You jest at this hour, in this place?" asked Halberd. "You have no fear of drowning?"

"Neither I nor you will die in this storm, young shaman. You think that only you might speak to the Gods, but Njord, God of the Sea, owes me much. Many treasures have I given him in tribute over the years and never have I asked for anything in return."

"Can our Gods hear our pleas so far from Northland?"

Halberd could scarcely accept what his ears told him. Halberd had never heard Mälar mention any God before. He was the least metaphysical man Halberd knew. Mälar never prayed.

Around them the wind surged, and Grettir's voice grew louder, singing sweet songs that made their limbs grow weary. Halberd longed to sleep. His head drooped and his hands loosened their grip on the ring of skins. Physical exhaustion overwhelmed him.

Suddenly his head rang. He looked to Mälar. The old man had boxed him in the ears. Mälar drew back his hand, ready to deliver another blow.

"Rouse yourself, Shaman!" he screamed. "The witch has power over you yet. Her spell enchants you to sleep. Drive her from your ears or die here and now."

Halberd realized in that moment he still carried love or lust for Grettir somewhere in his heart. If his heart was absolutely pure her spells could not affect him. But whose heart is absolutely pure?

Halberd raised his head into the wind and bellowed a long, meaningless shout. His drowsiness vanished. He clasped his doomed brother closer to him and hung onto the ring of skins.

"As for whether the Gods might hear us so far from our home," Mälar said, "now we shall see."

Mälar swam some distance from the life-ring of water skins. He trod water with his feet and raised his hands into the air.

"Hear me, Great Njord, Master of the Sea, Lord of the Waves and Wind, Keeper of All Boats and Ships," he called.

The wind did not increase, but Grettir's voice grew louder. A shrill keening filled the air. The witch fought to drown out Mälar's voice, to keep it from the ears of the Gods.

"Though every sea in the Known World have I sailed, though three times I was given up for drowned, though eight times two ships have sunk as I trod their decks, though all my brothers, save one, lie at the bottom of your watery fief, *never* have I petitioned you!"

The old man's voice rose proud and strong. It carried over the water and pierced the wind.

"Every time I seized booty by traveling over your deep roads, did I not drop part of it into your hands? Have I ever gained when you did not? Do not all the Gods in Aesir marvel at the wealth this mortal Mälar has brought to you?"

The wind dropped until it was just a breeze. Grettir's voice, sounding like the buzzing of distant bees, grew louder in reponse.

"Old man," cried Halberd, "Look behind you!"

Just above the white-breaking waves, two large yellow eyes arose. Two huge nostrils breathed steam across the stormy surface of the sea. The head and neck of a dragon broke the water and towered over the floating men. Water cascaded down its long, scaly neck. Waves broke over its shoulders, but it did not stir. It made no move to attack the men.

Usuthu, aware of the natural world as always, did not reach for his bow. He understood immediately that the beast posed no threat.

"It is Njord's eyes and ears, sent to hear my message," said Mälar.

Indeed, the creature gazed at Mälar with apparent concentration. It cocked its head in the driving rain. Despite its fangs, steaming breath and glittering scales, it resembled a dog at the fireplace, eager for its master to call it by name.

"Now, Great Njord, after a life at sea and in your service, I call for repayment for all my tribute. For me and my shipmates; and, wise Njord, for you as well. A witch, though whether she be immortal or mortal I cannot now say, manipulates that which is *yours* to *command!* If she gains sway over this remote sea in order to kill us miserable four, soon she may lay claim to other seas, vast and rich in treasure."

The waves slowly lessened. The sea fluttered and became calm as twilight on a summer eve. The buzzing of Grettir's ghostly voice faded away. The gray clouds opened and the sun broke at the horizon. Gulls circled above. The dragon sank back into the sea with a soft plop. As the clouds parted, the coastline came into view, near and rocky and lined with trees.

Mälar paddled back to Halberd.

"The land," he said, his face split by a huge smile, "lies this way."

"Will you not thank Njord for this favor?"

"It was no favor. It was a bargain. Woe to me if I ever ask for another. I have paid my entire life for this one service and I'll pay for the rest of it as well. Njord cares not for my thanks. He owed me. Now he does not. I owe him. Further, the witch Grettir presumed to rule over his territory."

"We have learned much of Grettir. She can control the seas, but only to a point. I believe she is still only a mortal. Her magic did not withstand the will of Njord for an instant. She could not even prevent my cries from reaching the god's ear."

"Old man, I do not possess your courage. Never have I addressed a God like a trader from the Land of Sand in a marketplace."

"Well, Halberd, if you survive to my age and that is still true, you may be able to do so. Once. Remember, the Gods admire presumption in a mortal. A small dose of presumption."

Halberd swam the unconscious body of Labrans over the ring of skins and hoisted him atop the largest one. Halberd clung to the ring and looked to Usuthu.

"When I came to cut you free," he asked, "why did you cross your arms over your chest? You looked like the stone statues of the dead kings near the pyramids in the Land of Sand."

"Because," answered the Mongol, bobbing up and down amid all their remaining supplies, "if I had use of my arms I would have grabbed you in fear, and both of us would be drowned."

"Why did you not pray to Bahaab Dahaabs to free you from the canoe, or to save you from the storm?"

"Bahaab Dahaabs cares not for my begging. If I am to die, then I shall die. I cannot ask him to alter the course of the world merely to prevent my stepping from this world into the next. Bahaab Dahaabs admires strength. I remained strong. I pray to him for guidance, not protection. When demons or immortals threaten me, then he may aid me, in order to make the fight a fair one."

"Usuthu," said Mälar, "tell us tales of your heathen philosophy at another, more leisurely time. Now, seize the ring of skins with your hands and kick with your feet, as we do. We must make shore before the witch sends her Skrælings after us again."

The three men rested their arms over the ring of skins and thrashed the flat sea with their feet. The spit of land grew larger. When they had kicked to within thirty feet of shore, Usuthu stood. The water reached almost to his chin. He stretched his back and raised his arms above his head. The shore here was sand and rock, protected from the elements by but a few windswept trees. Less than one league west, along the spit of land, a thick forest grew to the waterline.

Grinning with relief, Usuthu turned to his mates. "Well," he asked, "do you not wish to feel solid earth once again?"

"When you may stand we yet might drown," said Halberd. "Water that reaches your chin rises over my head by a foot. Here, drag this ring the remaining feet and lay Labrans on the shore."

Usuthu strode through the shallow water, towing the ring of skins effortlessly. Mälar and Halberd followed, slogging through the water until they were on shore. They sprawled on the sand, feeling their legs pump with blood once more. Usuthu hefted Labrans with no apparent effort and laid him upon his back on the sand.

The sun rose high, filling them with warmth and

drying their clothes. Halberd could feel the salt in his hair, on his skin, in his eyes and even under his fingernails. For the last three days he had not been aware of it once. He longed for a freshwater bath. He pulled his thick red hair with his wrinkled hands and scratched his scraggly beard.

"I am almost sick from lack of motion," Halberd said. "Longer journeys than this have I made, and never has the ground felt so odd."

"Because this time," Mälar told them, "you did not expect to touch it ever again. The feel of earth is so sweet it makes you sick."

"Did great explorers ever start a journey so ill-prepared as we?" asked Halberd. "No ponies, no ship, no crew, almost no food, cast onto a world we do not know, in search of a foe we may not see."

"That," rasped Mälar, "is truly adventure."

Their laughter echoed over the sand.

The Beach of Blood

The freezing rain slashed his face. Thunder cracked overhead and lightning followed instantly. His nose filled with the stench of sulphur. Halberd pulled his blanket around him once more. The hammock swung in the wind so wildly he could not sleep. Halberd raised his head to check on his companions. Usuthu had not moved since Halberd last opened his eyes, and Mälar stared into the night, searching for something in the screaming wind. Halberd settled back into his hammock. He could not dream if he could not sleep. But he could remember . . .

They had camped on the sand spit for two days and nights, regaining their strength. Mälar slept during the day, his head shrouded from the sunlight by his cloak. He lay awake on his back all night, learning this new sky of stars. He was making ready to guide them westward. Labrans awoke in due course and seemed not to remember his near-murder of the other three. He sat in a slumped heap, neither eating nor drinking nor answering any remark sent his way. While he slept, Halberd had disarmed him. Labrans did not remark on his missing weapons.

Those two days were easy, the first leisure they had enjoyed since leaving Northland months earlier. They took crabs from the bottom of the sea and speared fish in the shallows. At night they slept round a warming fire. No demons disturbed their slumber. No Skrælings sought their camp.

On the third dawn they lolled by their fire. Soon Halberd and Usuthu would scout this spit of land. Labrans sat on the sand, his head on his knees. He looked off to the west, where the spit joined the mainland some leagues distant.

"Grettir must have been sorely tested during that storm," said Halberd. "I believe it took much of her strength to produce it. I think the energy required to fight Njord has sapped her. We are left alone because she has been resting. It is an encouraging sign; if she were now immortal she would need no rest to counterattack us now. If she was strong we would be under seige at this moment."

"You underestimate the double-edged sword of her desires," answered Mälar. "You lust for her even as you crave her death. So, then, does she bear some lingering affection for you. Before she was a witch she was a woman. As a woman she loved you. With equal passion she hated you. You refused to demand that Valdane give her up and allow you to express your love. For that she will never forgive you. She is no longer a woman, but a woman's heart still beats in her breast.

"This affection does not lessen her hatred for you. It merely confuses her. She did not drag us around the Earth simply to see us filled with Skræling arrows. I believe that each attack we suffer amuses her. But your death, Halberd, the end of your young life, that is a different story.

"She is saving your death for her hands alone. She sends her foes upon us only to test our strength."

"How is it that a man with no wife knows so much of women's hearts?"

"Much," replied Mälar, "may be learned from a lifetime of observation from beyond the fire. One needn't participate to know the rules of the game. Indeed, women will speak more freely to a man who they know will be gone the next day. If they seek to woo him into marriage they may cloud his mind with deceit from their first meeting. My dealings with women have always been marked by bluntness, which is more than you can say, no matter what claims you lay for expertise."

"Bear this in mind, too," said Usuthu, "you stole Hrungnir from her and slew the dwarf who served Hel. Grettir may well have promised your soul to the Underworld God, as she delivered Valdane."

"If my soul is promised to Hel," said Halberd, "then I must be defeated in battle and enchanted for her to attain it. I must take great care. I shall not be defeated. But neither will I allow the witch to sap my soul's energy by making me a coward. If a battle looms, I shall fight it."

"You speak with the hot blood of the young," said Mälar, "but you speak foolishly. Let us consider our situation. We are three dragging a fourth, though we know he is a viper. We have neither shelter, herbs nor medicine. If one of us suffers a grave wound, how shall we heal him?"

"I know much healing," said Halberd, knowing as he spoke the direction Mälar pursued with this argument, "and Usuthu has powers as well."

"My boy, you miss my point. As three, we form a worthy fighting unit. I may navigate, no mortal fights like Usuthu and you have powers in the Nether Worlds. If one of us is slain, if we should lose any of these gifts, the surviving two are greatly weakened."

"And therefore?" asked Halberd, smiling at this old man who loved the role of teacher.

Usuthu, who also knew the upcoming answer, looked away, deep in thought.

"And therefore, Shaman, we may face challenges which in other worlds and other wars we would fight with glee. Here we may be forced to flee like rabbits. We must not attack any foe with blind courage. If you wish revenge you must live to attain it. For the good of all, you must temper your bravery with reservation. You will ensure that we fight no fight that we may not win. As you captain this crew, so do you assume responsibility for it."

"Bag of wind you may be" said Halberd, "but you are right. I will not jeopardize us by my hot-bloodedness. But if I see Grettir in my grasp, I will slay her."

"So shall we all, Halberd. So shall we all."

"Then," rose a screeching, unearthly wail, "slay me now!"

Halberd spun on the sand, reaching for his sword. Mälar raised his head, too shocked to move. Usuthu was up with the reflexes of a cat, dashing across the sand toward his bow.

Standing atop a slight grade to the west stood Grettir. Her arms were spread wide, her eyes glowed red and feral. Her white gown was sculpted to her body by the gentle breeze, and her nipples and dark hair showed through the fine fabric.

It did not matter that her eyes promised only bloodshed; her body was exquisite. Her lean, supple strength showed through the light robe, and her skin glowed. She parted her mouth slightly and her perfectly white, even teeth gleamed in the morning sun.

As always, Halberd had only to look at her and his manhood rose. If she came forward and put her arms around him, Halberd would lay her gently on the beach and pound himself into her until the sun fell from the sky. She provoked little love, but uncontrollable lust. He shook his head to drive out his desire. Her spell over him was strong.

His urge for vengeance was stronger.

Grettir's long blond hair was woven about her head in a witch's braid. She bore an oddly painted shield of animal hide and a single long lance. Hanging about her neck was the horn of an oxen. Red sealing wax closed off the wide end. She smirked at the sight of the warriors scrambling for their weapons.

"You wanted me," she cried, her voice raising the hair on Halberd's neck and sending bumps down his arms, "and now I am come."

Halberd felt suddenly cold, as if winter had descended with all its frozen power. He longed to raise his sword, but his limbs were frozen.

Usuthu, kneeling on the sand, fired an arrow without hesitation. Grettir glanced at the missile in mid-flight and barely moved her shield. The arrow passed into the shield without a sound. The shaft vanished into the painted hide, and no arrow appeared on the other side.

Labrans raised his head from his knees to watch the flight of the arrow. As it disappeared, he clapped his hands like a small child and grinned with delight.

"Do not waste your efforts," Usuthu cried. "She is not corporeal. Her evil magic controls this apparition from some other place. She is not here."

Halberd, bearing his broadsword before him, looked to the Jewel of Kyrwyn-Coyne to confirm Usuthu's words. The jewel glowed brightly. Mälar fired another arrow.

Grettir threw back her head and laughed in a gentle, seductive tone. It was the chuckle of an lascivious schoolgirl, not the leer of a witch. At this arrow she merely pointed the tip of her lance. The arrow disappeared in midair.

Labrans rolled on his back in the sand, laughing hysterically. Tears rolled down his cheeks.

"Silence, fool!" the witch hissed. She pointed

her lance at Labrans. Vomit burst from his mouth. Blood poured from his nostrils. He rolled forward onto his knees, clutching himself as long gouts of green half-digested food spurted forth. His face contorted in agony.

"Wherever *I* may be," the witch spoke softly in an effort to gain control of herself, "my warriors live." She shook the oxhorn. "Made from the blood of the crew of Valdane and my spittle, which has given them life anew. Behold, and make your way west as you please."

Halberd dropped his broadsword into the sand and reached to his back, to the holster in which Hrungnir rested. He yanked the stone knife up and held it before him.

"Come closer, demon," Halberd called, his heart pounding. It was his first chance to address the witch since the dream of his brother's death. "Walk up to the point of my knife, that I might kiss you as I cut out your heart."

"Ahh," she answered in a voice as sweet as a thousand gentle kisses, "that knife is not yours but Hel's, and she has commended it to me. I suggest you return it to its owner lest you stir her wrath."

Despite himself, Halberd took one step forward, the knife lowering. Mälar seized his arm and held him fast.

"Oh, you will not come to me?" Grettir moaned. "Then let my soldiers come to you. If you defeat them, travel west. We shall meet again, sleeping or waking."

With that, she punctured the red wax with the

tip of her lance. She inverted the oxhorn and shook it. Bright drops of blood flew forth, and where each struck the ground a Northman warrior sprang up, armed and armored. Worse, each demon looked like brave Kvasir and other members of Valdane's crew.

It was Kvasir's ghost who had told Halberd how Grettir had slain him and his fellows on Vinland. Kvasir had warned Halberd that Grettir had stolen the blood from their dead bodies. That blood, mixed with the spittle of the witch, had borne new life. Life that did not live. Life that was undead.

The demons bore the countenances of men Halberd had known since his childhood, men whose mutilated bodies he had burned and then buried on Vinland. Their faces were the faces of friends, but there were no eyes in their fiendish heads. Empty sockets stared at Halberd, freezing his blood.

"These are not your friends," whispered Mälar fiercely. "Your friends are dead and perhaps in Aasgard. These are demons made of blood and spittle. You know them not. Cast aside your sympathy and harden your heart."

Halberd turned his eyes from the black holes in the heads of the advancing warriors and looked at Grettir. She tilted her head sweetly and made his manhood ache with one final, seductive burning look, then she vanished back into the air. A wisp of smoke marked her departure. Scorched ground marked where she had stood.

The approaching warriors numbered between twenty and thirty. They were armed with clubs and axes, maces and broadswords. None carried bows or arrows. When the brave men whose blood had created these fiends had been slain on Vinland, they had held only weapons for combat at close quarters. The demons bore the same arms their living counterparts had held at the moments of their deaths.

Mälar moved to Halberd's side and dragged him beside Usuthu. The black Mongol launched a flight of arrows. The three watched the arrows' flights with great interest. The demons made no move to evade nor raised their shields. Usuthu had fired five arrows in the blink of an eye. He held an arrow to his bowstring as he waited to gauge the effect of the first flight.

One demon, taken in the chest, fell to the ground and was pinned there. His arms and legs still moved freely. Another, shot through the neck, moved forward, though his limbs were hampered. Those struck in the legs could no longer walk, but others continued unimpeded.

"The arrows do whatever damage they might to muscle," said Halberd as the small army grew nearer and nearer, "but they do not kill. Shoot, then, to disable and I shall move among them with Hrungnir and slay these poor souls, who have been dead for weeks.

"I believe only magic may attack magic. Our swords will not kill them, but Hrungnir's power might."

"Stay here, Usuthu, and fill them with your shafts," said Mälar. "I cherish the chance to swing

57

a blade. I'll draw some to the south and chop them into bits. Halberd, give me your ax."

"Beware, Mälar," said Halberd. He pulled his iron-headed battle-ax from the holster he wore on his left side. Made by the smiths on the Guardian Rock at the entrance to the Inland Sea, his axe was perfectly balanced and razor-sharp. "I fear only Hrungnir may actually kill them. Cut off their legs or arms, but do not bother trying for the mortal wound."

Halberd extended the ax to Mälar, butt first. Mälar hefted the ax, tested its balance and smiled grimly.

Usuthu said nothing. He shook his quiver until all the arrows were spilled on the ground beside him. Halberd, anxious not to get in their path, circled the Mongol and made for the water's edge.

Eight or nine of the untouched demons headed for him. Halberd shifted Hrungnir to his left hand and clutched his broadsword in his right. The Jewel of Kyrwyn-Coyne glowed so brightly it distracted him. As always, the feel of Hrungnir in his hand filled him with power and confidence. The stone pyramid bore great and unearthly strength. It had slain Valdane. One day it would slay Grettir.

The thought of revenge filled Halberd's heart with bloodlust. He moved swiftly toward the demons.

Halberd splashed through ankle-deep water, where the sand was most firm. The eyeless warriors approached him from the deeper sand and could move less rapidly. Halberd dashed at the first demon. Halberd swung his broadsword in a downward arc at the fearsome creature's leg. The demon answered with a wild swing of his mace, which Halberd ducked under. Low to the ground, he swung again at the demon's right leg and this time send it flying from the creature's body. It hit the water's surface with a dull splat. The demon fell into the sand. Blood pumped out of his twitching stump. He swung at Halberd even though he could not stand up. The demon was immobilized, legless, yet unhurt.

Two had closed on Halberd. They were atop him. He crouched on the blood-sprayed sand, recovering from the strong swing of his sword at ankle height. His sword stroke had carried his right arm across his body. His sword tip rested on the sand as he knelt. The two demons, moving without haste, raised their swords over their heads. Apparently they could not move as swiftly as a living man. Their black eye sockets stared coldly forward. Halberd uncoiled, leaning upward as he swung his great blade back-handed across his body, hacking upward toward the sky.

He severed the heads from both demons, and saw from the corner of his eye both bleeding heads soar into the blue sky and land at the water's edge. Headless, the two bodies groped their way down the shoreline, swinging their swords into the air. They were not mortally wounded.

Halberd shoved his sword through the chest of the next demon and simultaneously swung Hrungnir left-handed toward the face of another. The sword thrust, though fatal to any mortal, barely slowed this foul spawn of Niflheim. A club blow on his shoulder sent Halberd sprawling onto the sand and he rolled over in a fast somersault, stopping abruptly with his sword blade in front of him. It was the first fighting trick Valdane had ever taught him.

The demon who struck Halberd raced forward. He thrust himself onto Halberd's suddenly stationary blade. Halberd drove Hrungnir to the hilt into the demon's back. He yanked his broadsword out of the creature's chest and shuffled backward. His head up and his sword before him, Halberd scanned the field of battle.

The three eyeless monsters whom Halberd had struck with Hrungnir had vanished. They were nowhere to be seen. The one with no leg rolled to and fro on the sand, trying to stand. The two lacking heads were far down the beach, with no sense of where the battle lay.

The remaining two demons squirmed on the beach, pinned to the sand by Usuthu's arrows. Their arms and legs thrashed clumsily as they tried to pull free of the huge bolts that held them fast. Usuthu and Mälar were wading into the remaining force, swinging their sword and ax wildly, like guides chopping a path through thick forest. Limbs flew from the demons and soon all lay on the sand amid a welter of arms and legs and eyeless, helmeted heads.

Halberd was splashed with blood. Hrungnir was coated with gore, none of it human. Halberd moved slowly along the beach, driving the dripping stone pyramid into the chests of each demon, twisting and turning, then wrenching the mystical weapon from their armored chests.

Each spasmed horribly when struck. Each made no sound, but the crack of their breaking ribs and the sticky grip of their ruptured chests made every finishing thrust more horrible than Halberd could bear. As the stone knife did its work, as the last unliving breath passed out of each demon's mouth, the creatures simply vanished. Only their armor, helmets and weapons remained. Arrows sticking from the sand marked the place where they had fallen. Halberd was too overcome by his grisly task to feel surprise.

When the six before him had returned to the void whence they had sprung, Halberd moved up the beach to the cluster of demons Usuthu had claimed with his bow.

"Usuthu," asked Halberd, "why is it so much worse to kill these demons than to slay honest warriors in a fair fight?"

"Have strength, my brother," the Mongol said, laying a huge blood-soaked hand on Halberd's shoulder. "She would sap you with this horrible task and make you feel pity. Feel none. Only you may wield the stone knife, so only you may finish these miserable empty shells. Harden yourself and go to the slaughter. I'll retrieve the headless ones."

Usuthu strode down the beach, his curved bronze blade throwing drops of blood on the already soaked sand. Mälar knelt on the sand, exhausted. He drank deeply from a water skin. Halberd's ax, covered with bloody hair, stood in the sand beside him, held upright by its blade buried in the beach.

Labrans lay on his side, soaked in his own vomit, spent and wracked by his cramps and bleeding.

"Don't let Labrans die," said Halberd. "When you are full, give him a drink. I'll dispatch these beasts. After we've eaten and rested, we move. I won't sleep in this place."

Mälar nodded, gasping for breath.

"This is not glorious battle," Mälar spat, reaching for every breath with a rattle in his chest. "This is butchery designed to tire us and make us yearn for home. I am too old for such urges. I do not and shall not yearn for home, wherever that is. I yearn to be in the Unknown World and so I am. Any, witch or woman, who dares to put me through an ordeal like this will pay. When we find her, I will not allow you to kill her alone. Here and now, I demand my piece of vengeance."

The old sailor spoke with vehemence. Halberd, as always, drew strength from the endless reserve of toughness that had carried Mälar to the farthest corners of the Known World. Such anger in the face of this bloodshed was bracing.

"You will share, old man," Halberd said quietly.

Vengeance might be shared, but none could share his chore. Halberd went from thrashing body to thrashing body: this one lacking legs, this one cut near in twain by a slashing sword, this one with arms hanging by threads, all dressed as Northmen and all with no eyes and no expression on their undead faces. Halberd plunged Hrungnir deep into the chests of all, bursting their undead yet pumping hearts and dispatching each into thin air.

When the beach was empty of demons, yet rattling full of discarded swords and empty helmets, Halberd sat. Usuthu strode the sand, yanking his arrows out of the dirt and straightening each shaft with his massive hands. Mälar sat with splayed legs, Halberd's ax between them. Mälar slowly and deliberately stropped the blade with a whetstone. The ghastly screech of the stone on the blade echoed over the blood-soaked beach.

"Alive or undead," he said "these soldiers are made of bone as tough as ours. All this hacking chopped great pits into your blade. I must make it ready for the next attack. It is a fine weapon. Its balance is perfect."

"It ought to be, for what it cost. You need not prattle on. I will learn from your example," said Halberd wearily. "My heart will harden as needed. I will fight this fight as the merciless war it must be."

"Rest easy, Shaman. You killed Skrælings on Vinland not because they were barbarians and strangers, but because they wanted to kill you. Likewise, these monsters sought the same goal. These demons resembled your friends. To kill them has cost you dearly. Grettir is a master tactician. She knows these creatures could not stop us. She sent them to steal the goodness from your heart. Do not become too unfeeling too soon. Your sweeter nature will protect you from the witch as surely as your sword arm protects you from the Skrælings."

"You are an unpredictable source of wisdom, Mälar. You swing me in one direction and then another. The path you describe may be too narrow to walk and still remain sane."

"Maybe so," said Mälar, "but you had better try."

Usuthu dropped his full quiver on the sand. He sank down next to his fellow explorers and gazed over the bloody sand.

"No thoughts of the Waking World may guide us in such a fight," he said gravely. "We fight magic and so need to gain magic to be as strong as our foe.

"We'll move our camp into the woods before nightfall. Then you, Halberd, must seek succor from Ishlanawanda and I must return in trance to the Steppes of my people. Magic have I faced, but never evil with such force. We must find our path through this Unknown World. As we go, we must not allow the witch to rob us of our identities as men of battle and honor. I can consult my heart no longer. I need the wisdom of others."

Ignoring the weapons, helmets and armor littering the beach the Northmen gathered up what remained of their possessions. Their journey into the Unknown World began with a single step westward. They remained low on the beach, near the water, keeping clear ground between the thick forest and themselves.

They walked without speaking. The day passed without a spoken word. An hour before twilight, Mälar, exercising his right as navigator, called the halt.

"The forest moves too close to the beach to provide a clear field across which to fire," he said.

"We'll move into the woods now, find a clearing and make our camp."

Usuthu turned into the woods. Mälar waded into the sea with his sword, searching for crabs or bottom-clinging shellfish. Halberd took Labrans by the arm and led him along the path forged by Usuthu.

Soon their fire roared under the darkening sky. They plucked scorching crabs from the flames and ate their fill. The day's grim action receded.

"What make you, Usuthu," Halberd asked, "of the shape of this spit? Can you place our camp along its length?"

"It curves outward in a curious spiral," Usuthu began. "The eastern tip of this spiral points dead north. For several leagues this tip runs north–south, then it intersects with the east–west arm of the spit. These arms form the spiral, which, I believe, juts from the eastern coast of this world. The shape of this land mass is familiar to me, but I cannot name it."

"The shape," spake Mälar, "is that of a fighting hook or a grappling iron, with the top laid against the continent and the hook curving east and north from the coast."

"I have never seen these implements," said Usuthu.

"He's right," said Halberd, describing such a hook with his hands in the cool night air. "Where on this hook do we now rest?"

"We are a bit west of the middle. Three days' walk will take us to the coast. Once we reach the mainland our route depends on Grettir. And on your visions.

"I have slept these last two days. My nights I've passed reading the stars. I am not tired; I will not sleep tonight. You, Halberd, must dream. I'll stand guard. Tomorrow, however, we may not travel. I will be asleep.

"You must stand guard alone," said Usuthu. "I will not be here to aid you." The Mongol took up his sword and stepped into the thick woods.

"Hm!" sniffed Mälar. "Is he night hunting? Scouting the Skrælings? Tired of my good conversation?"

"He goes," said Halberd, "to fall into a deep trance, as he did on the ship. While in this trance he sends his spirit back to the Great Steppes, to ride with the people of his tribe. What he learns there remains his secret."

"Sleep, Shaman. We cannot travel without guidance."

Halberd removed his armor. He pulled Hrungnir from its holster and clutched the knife tightly. He feared to enter the Dream world without it. He rolled into his furs. His broadsword rested beside him.

Mälar sat by the fire, appearing to stare mindlessly into the coals. Halberd knew that the old man was aware of every sound and scent. At the first unfamiliar sign Mälar would give the alarm. His sword rested on a log beside him. Halberd's ax leaned against his drawn-up knee.

Mälar returned Halberd's watchful gaze without emotion.

"Sleep," he said.

Halberd closed his eyes. His heart pounded at the thought of seeing Ishlanawanda again. He took a single deep breath and was instantly asleep.

Halberd walks along a narrow path through the forest. This forest bears no resemblance to the coastal woods of the Unknown World. Here the trees are well speard, with high branches. No tangled underbrush grows. The ground underfoot is deeply carpeted with pine needles. Dappled shafts of sunlight reach down through the trees and strike the forest floor. The atmosphere is one of complete and utter calm.

He is near the village of Ishalanawanda.

He climbs a small hill and there, lying before him, is the village.

The river loops across the gentle landscape in great, wide bends. The village sits in one bend. The dwellings are odd tents, wide at the bottom and narrow at the top. A cluster of tent poles protrudes, from a hole at the top. The tents are made of animal hide scraped clean and painted in story telling pictures. One depicts a hunt, another the birth of a child, another herds of huge four-footed beasts with enormous shoulders, black fur manes, tiny eyes and short curved horns.

The Skrælings who live in this village greatly resemble those who chased the Northmen from the shore of the Unknown World. Their braided hair is long and black. Their skin is an appealing reddish-brown. Yet these Skrælings are taller and more regal in bearing. They move with graceful dignity. Even their children show a natural grace as they leap about the village playing war games with tiny bows and clubs.

Halbard watches the village for a moment before he descends the hill. Everything seems at peace. He follows the path which he trod in earlier dreams. He leaves the clearing at the crest of the hill and re-enters the forest. The path winds through the trees once more. At the edge of the trees he stops. He knows he can go no farther.

The conical tent nearest him bears a painting unlike all the others. On it is depicted a large white-skinned man with a full red beard and thick red hair. He bears the pyramid knife before him. At his side is painted a long-haired Skræling woman. This is the tent of Ishlanawanda.

The tent flap is thrown aside. She steps into the sunlight and sees Halberd standing at the entrance to the village. She runs lightly across the field between them as swiftly as a deer. She is tall and slender, yet strong. Her black hair hangs down her back to her waist and blows free in the wind as she races towards him. Her skin is brown and smooth, and her deep black eyes are filled with love.

Halberd's heart leaps at the sight of her. Grettir may be his profane and damning lust, but Ishlanawanda is his sacred and saving love.

She fills his heart with peace and contentment. Since she first appeared in his dreams, Ishlanawanda has brought an end to the restlessness in Halberd's soul. He extends his arms to catch her, forgetting in his love the restrictions that bind them.

They have never touched.

When she is within arm's reach she stops, a horrified look on her face.

"Why do you bring Hrungnir?" she cries. "I thought today you would enter my village at last."

"I am not safe from the witch," Halberd replies. His heart breaks at the anticipation in her eyes, the way her breath comes short when she nears him, as does his when he sees her.

"She could find me in the Dream World with ease," Halberd continues. "Hrungnir guarantees my safety. Only its power keeps her at bay."

"There is other power, Shaman," the Skræling replies. "You have not attempted to learn it. You must. We will not touch until you discard this weapon when you enter the Dream World."

"I came seeking that knowledge from you, my love," Halberd says gently. "I sought you every night as we sailed the coast of the Unknown World. I searched for your village but I could not find it. The Skrælings drove us down the coast like animals. Only today have we made a camp worthy of the name."

"I know of your ordeal. I have missed you with all my heart. I could not lead you to me. My elders denied you access to our village. Our love angers them greatly."

"But you sought me, Ishlanawanda. You made the first contact. Your people must understand that I mean you no harm. Did I not slay Fallat?"

"Yes. Fallat came here only to do evil. He had powers we could not resist, as does Grettir, at times. He was the first man from the Waking World ever to find this place, but he was not really a man. He had lived for thousands of years and absorbed so much knowledge that he more closely resembled a spirit. We allowed him to enter. Why not? We concealed certain things he should not know, and he let us be. His pride blinded him. He fell in love with himself simply because he located our village. He never pursued the deeper questions.

"But you, you slew this beast. You had powers greater than his. You terrified my elders and they sent me to spy upon you, to see if you were more dangerous to us than this man we had known for centuries.

"As you are gifted in your world, I am gifted in mine. So I was chosen as the spy. I could travel farther into what you in the Waking World consider civilized lands. Now that you walk upon the Unknown World you will learn what civilization truly means. The men of this world may lack arrowheads of metal or written words, but they guard their knowledge jealousy. Much is hidden here. Peer beneath the surface of every encounter. The words unspoken carry the greatest importance."

She pauses and each gazes into their true love's eyes.

"I failed as a spy," Ishlanawanda says. "I felt love in my heart the moment I saw you—"

"And I you," Halberd interrupts.

". . . and so I revealed myself to you," she continues, "and aided you in your search for this continent. Now you have come. None in my village believed you would. They do not know what to do with you. You bear Hrungnir. You are forbidden to enter our village so long as you do. You must learn to travel in my world without its protection."

"Tell me how," Halberd says. "Reveal to me its secrets, that I may discard it and come to you as your lover"

"I will not! I cannot!" Ishlanawanda speaks with a force that Halberd has not yet seen. "You must learn its power on your own, by your own cunning and wisdom. You cannot control the knife of stone unless you understand it. This is a quest no one may make in your stead."

"And when I have learned to travel here without Hrungnir," Halberd says, "'and without fearing the witch, will I then be able to enter your village?"

"That," Ishlanawanda says with great sadness, "I cannot say. If you had come today without weapons, perhaps. Hear me well, Halberd, you are the love of my heart and I will hold you in my arms if I may, but perhaps I may not.

"Can you imagine how few mortals, through all the years our worlds have existed, ever stood where you now stand? Any idea? Fewer than five, my love, in tens of thousands of years. Fewer than five.

"No man or woman from the Waking World has ever remained in this village for any length of time. No man or woman of the Dream World has ever touched a mortal from the Waking World. What will happen when we do touch? Are our Worlds intended to be bridged?

"You and I know we are destined to be lovers. My elders do not. They fear, with good reason, what will happen if we are lovers. What if I am made with child? What would this child be? Where would lie the proper world of its birth?

"I cannot live in the Waking World. I live here, in the Dream World of this continent. My people want for nothing. We battle our enemies in this region, but that is the way of all worlds; warriors must have war. But we are at peace with the spirits of our world.

"You, my love, are never in harmony with the spirits in your world. You travel merely for vengeance, for blood. Your own actions with the wife of your brother stain you with that same blood. You are not pure of heart."

"No mortal," speaks Halberd, "is completely pure of heart."

"I am learning that," she replies. "I trust you. I love you. I welcome you to my world. My elders do not. You must prove your good intentions. You must learn how to travel without Hrungnir. You possess vast spiritual gifts. More than you know. Believe in your power. Do not believe in trinkets which fate has dropped in your path."

"Your elders are wise," Halberd answers. "There must be balance between the Waking World and the World of Dreams. All I care about is my love for you. But I will be faithful to my powers as a shaman. I respect both worlds. I will ask for no more aid in this matter. This I vow. But I know nothing of the Skræling way. Can you guide me?"

"What would you know?"

"Why did they drive us away? Why do they fear us so?"

"Because they fear Grettir. They mistook her for the coming of a prophecy. They bowed down to her golden hair. She enslaved the first three villages she came to and left them in ruins. She travels with a strong force of warriors.

"Every village awaits an attack by Grettir and her servants. When she was treated as a goddess she warned all of your coming. When she showed herself to be demonic she promised vengeance on any who aided you. The tribes which know Grettir will not help you."

"Perhaps," says Halberd, "I can move west more rapidly than she, and make contact with those not yet encouraged to kill me."

"To kill you is forbidden. She wants you and your friends seized and held for her pleasure."

"Where is she now?"

"She moves west and north. My elders fear that she makes for the Thundering Falls on the shore where the Lakes You Cannot See Across meet. The falls are a place of power. It is far. She moves rapidly, plundering as she goes. She scorches the earth in her path."

"Will your elders permit you to show me the way?"

"Perhaps. It depends on your actions. They might

decide to set you upon Grettir. To let each of you slay the other. If they choose that strategy they will be delighted for me to guide you."

"Can they not see that the enemy of Grettir is their friend?"

"Grettir is strong, but we do not fear her as we did Fallat. We can keep her at bay. Many battles in the Waking World do not affect us. The battle between you and Grettir may well be one. Such a battle could be to our benefit. Today there exist two mortals who are able to find our village. After your battle there would only be one, at most."

"Those are hard words but fair," Halberd says. "I long for you, Ishlanawanda, with all my heart. Our love is fated. This I know. I will do what I must."

Ishlanawanda's dark eyes shine with love.

"I can aid you in small ways," she says. "I will guide you to the falls."

"Can we sail on an inland river or sea from the east to the west?"

"No. Your path lies overland, over mountains and through thick forest."

"How may we communicate with the Skrælings?"

"There are many tribes. All have their own language. Most are well versed in the language of gestures."

"Are there any we must fear over others?"

"Beware the Eerhahkwoi. They wear their hair in a narrow upright line from the front of their heads to the rear. Many have been slain by Grettir. Many others serve in her army."

ON THE SHOULDERS OF GIANTS

Ishlanawanda looks over her shoulder at her village. No children play now. Standing at her tent are a group of older Skræling men. Their power and dignity show in their faces even at a distance.

"I have said all that I may say," Ishlanawanda speaks quickly. "Now you must go."

"Is there nothing more you may tell me?"

Halberd steps nearer to his love. As he does, she and the village behind her move away from him by the same distance that he moves forward.

She looks over her shoulder once more. She turns back to face Halberd.

"Hrungnir and the Jewel of Kyrwyn-Coyne are linked. You must learn the origin of the knife to understand the jewel. Now go."

Halberd's love whirls away and runs back to her village. One of the elders holds the tent flap for her and she ducks inside. The old men follow her in. Clearly, they will council with her and learn of Halberd's words.

Halberd turns back down the path. The last time he walked these woods Grettir attacked him. Only her fear of Hrungnir kept her at bay. Halberd watches the trees with care.

He climbs the hill overlooking Ishlanawanda's village. Children play again between the tents. Women sit by fires cooking as men return from the hunt. Canoes fill the gentle river. The Skrælings in the canoes spear fish and splash one another with their paddles. Their playful shouts sound throughout the woods. Life in the village seems unbearably peaceful.

Halberd stands on the outside looking in. This world of peace is not his. He is a man of blood, of war, of exploration and of vengeance. Love will come, when it does, only in his dreams.

Halberd awakes.

The Eerhahkwoi and the Bear

The dream faded from memory. Halberd's rendez-vous with Ishlanawanda had been several nights before. He had not attempted to contact her since. For good reason. He had barely slept.

The storm roared on. Soaked to the skin, Halberd could only wait until morning. He reviewed every memory of that dream; the glow of love in Ishlana-wanda's eye, the slight movement of her smooth, sleek body beneath her deerhide garment, the yearn-ing in her voice.

Halberd swung his gaze to the sky. Some light-ness glowed here and there through breaks in the clouds. He looked out over the hammock toward the ground. The giant serpent was gone. So was the body of the Skræling. One had fed the other. So be it.

Morning meant movement. But morning was still some time away. Halberd turned on one side in the swinging hammock and wrapped his arms around himself. He cast his thoughts back to the camp on the beach . . .

. . . When he had awoken from his dream, Usuthu and Mälar had been waiting by the fire. It was full light. They chewed dried fish, watching him with care. Labrans sat against a tree, his eyes far, far away.

"Labrans," spake Halberd from his sleeping furs, "can you hear me? Do you know where you are?"

His brother did not speak, but rocked back and forth against the tree, his mouth hanging open.

"He is utterly possessed," said Mälar. "I think the witch fills his head with new instructions. He cannot hear us. Speak freely."

"A trek awaits us," said Halberd. "We must cross mountains and forests, and there is no waterway upon which to sail. Grettir leads a small army of Skrælings. She seeks a giant waterfall. This falls lies in a place of power. We must reach it before her."

"And your love?" asked Mälar, his eyes gleaming with mirth. "How fares your affairs of the heart?"

"There is no love," Halberd answered. "None at all until I can travel to her world without Hrungnir."

"How will you do that?" At last Usuthu spoke.

"When we make a true camp, I will dream once more and visit my mother. She, if anyone, will know the secrets of this knife."

Usuthu looked away. "Perhaps," he said.

"Eat," said Mälar. "We start walking when you are full."

"Do neither of you wish to know how far we must walk?"

"As far as it is, we shall walk that far and no farther," answered Mälar. "After we kill the witch we walk back. What does it matter?"

"After we have walked a month," said Halberd, "and we have another month of walking before us tell me if it matters."

As they wound their way through the trees, Mälar addressed them in a booming voice. "Northmen are men of ships, Mongols are men of horseback, yet here we are, landlocked and afoot. A great adventure, hundreds of leagues of unknown forest and mountains and only our feet for transport. We will not grow fat on this journey, my friends."

"Must we stay on the path, Mälar?" asked Halberd. "A Skræling path means eventually we shall encounter Skrælings."

"Well," came the shouted reply, "what shall we do to fight the boredom of walking if not fight?"

"What has Usuthu told you, old man, to make you so cheery?"

"I'll not betray a confidence, my boy, ask him yourself."

Usuthu stepped up the path until he was side by side with Halberd. As they spoke they strode briskly. Labrans lagged behind Mälar, but never so far back that the men were out of sight.

"The old man mocks you," said Usuthu. "I speak to no one in my trances. No one sees me. I send my spirit to be among my people, to ride my good horse and to renew my strength. Mälar awoke ready for adventure, so he shouts. In that way he is much like your father."

"Aye," Halberd said. "Mälar, you lead the way from the rear. Is this how much confidence you have in our route?"

"I know only that we must move due west and then north. Give me greater detail as you learn it."

"That I shall," Halberd said.

They marched all day. The path wound through thick woods. The ground underfoot changed from springy sand to hard clay to rich black soil. Rocks filled the path. The beginning of spring was near. The air was cool but not cold, and the sky was clear.

Game abounded. Deer crossed their path, unafraid. Large elk roamed the hills and the loud cough of bears could be heard, as well as the hoarse growl of great cats.

In the middle of the day Mälar held up his hand. They froze. They listened.

A loud snapping of twigs and rustling of leaves announced that something moved toward them. Each brought up his weapon. Mälar had apparently adopted Halberd's ax. He had not offered to return it. Halberd yanked his broadsword from its scabbard and Usuthu nocked an arrow in his bow. As always, his black arms moved with a quickness that defied belief. Halberd could discern only a blur. The three warriors surrounded Labrans. They stood with their backs touching, each facing a different direction.

They waited, poised. Labrans lay between them, curled into a ball, his thumb in his mouth. He had dropped into that pose the instant he stopped moving.

The crackling and snapping of twigs and branches grew louder. Usuthu craned his neck to see over the thick vegetation. The plants grew over the height of Halberd's and Mälar's head. Usuthu drew back his bowstring and let fly. In the distance sounded a thump! as the arrow struck home. Instantly another arrow was ready.

"What do you see?" Halberd whispered.

"Mälar," said Usuthu, in a voice too calm to be calm, "gaze about you. Are there any trees that we might climb? Nearby?"

"No."

"Then slide your ax into my hand. Do not move quickly. When I jump, follow me with your sword drawn."

"Usuthu, are we fighting man or animal? Spirit or flesh?"

"Old man, I have never seen the like. I will answer your question when it is dead."

Moving as stealthily as he could, Mälar passed the ax into Usuthu's hand. As his hand closed around the haft, the Mongol sprang into the bushes, the blade high overhead. Halberd crashed behind him, following his trail of broken branches. Mälar pulled his sword from its ornate scabbard and leapt from the path. Labrans lay without moving, his eyes rolling about in his skull.

Halberd raced through the bushes after Usuthu. Branches whipped into his eyes and thorns tore at his sides. He could see Usuthu ahead, apparently standing on a rock, chopping down with wide, slashing strokes. The rising ax threw blood and chunks of flesh above his head.

Halberd came up behind the Mongol. Usuthu seemed to be standing on a huge log. The top of the log came up to Halberd's chest. The log was green and gold and covered with scales. Halberd whirled to look at Usuthu. As the ax fell again the log whipped sideways and knocked Halberd back into the onrushing Mälar. They fell in a heap in the thick woods.

They untangled and regained their feet. The log lay still. Dark, viscous blood formed a puddle beneath it. Usuthu rose from the bushes beside the log. Halberd's ax, coated with scales, dripped the same fluid.

"This, my brothers," said Usuthu, "is the largest snake I ever beheld." His face contorted with disgust. He wiped the ax on a handful of leaves and returned it to Mälar. He started back toward the path.

Halberd and Mälar examined the creature. Its head was a bloody pulp hacked into bits. They could not push through the thick underbrush to find where the snake ended.

"What a beast!" exclaimed Halberd. "Its head is larger than you, Mälar."

"Aye. If these brutes are common, we've slept our last night on the ground."

They picked their way back to the path. Halberd bled from numerous scratches and Mälar had suffered a sword gash when they collided.

"Henceforth," pronounced Usuthu, "I'll flee before I'll kill another of those. I cannot bear snakes. Snakes larger than the ship on which I crossed the miserable sea . . . well. Dragons I do not fear, but snakes. Agh!"

"My brother," said Halberd, amazed to find something on earth which upset the Mongol, "that snake is not quite so large as our dragon-ship."

"Perhaps," shot back the Mongol, "but can you deny that it dwarfs our canoe, in which we sailed for days?"

"Ahh," said Halberd. "In truth, no."

"Allow me, Usuthu," said Mälar, a huge grin splitting his face, "to carve you a generous steak from the flank of your prey. You have slain it, so you warrant the first bite."

Mälar raised the ax and turned towards the snake.

"Hold, old man!" shouted Usuthu.

"Do you not cherish the rich, oily taste of snake, my boy?" Mälar asked sweetly.

"Thank you for your consideration," the Mongol answered with grave formality, "but my early meal of dried fish has left me with no more appetite."

The Mongol swung back onto the path and started walking.

"That," said Mälar, "answers your question about leaving the path. We dare not walk in these woods."

The path wound on. They saw no one, found no tracks in the black dirt and spoke little. As nightfall neared they climbed the trees nearest the path, made for the highest branches and slept in relative ease, their cloaks serving as hammocks. Labrans, for all his insanity, climbed easily and without aid. It cheered them to see that he was not physically impaired. Perhaps they still might call upon his aid in a fight.

By first light they were back on the trail. By noon they had found the village.

Mälar, leading the way, stopped in his tracks. He held up a warning hand. They dropped low and slid next to the old man. They had seen the clearing, but they did not know what it meant.

They were looking down on the village from a grass-rimmed lip about three man-heights above it. A freshwater stream bubbled at the opposite end of the village. There was only one Skræling in sight, an old, old man. His long hair was gray and matted. He rocked back and forth, chanting in a gutteral tone and whacking the ground with a small stone hatchet.

The old man sat in the mist of desolation. What had once been a village was now ash. Everything had been burned to the ground. A few blackened spars and narrow tree trunks bound together tilted crazily. No animals moved, no cook-fire blazed. Here and there blackened arms and legs jutted up from a knee-deep sea of shifting ash. Resting against one standing tree was a perfectly white skeleton picked free of all flesh.

The old man beat the ground with his hatchet. "Huh, huh, huh, huh," he chanted over and over. He did not raise his head. He did not notice the ash that covered him. He did not see the Northmen.

"I have seen such destruction," Usuthu whispered, "when I rode with the armies of the Great Khan. We scourged the cities of our enemies in this manner. We burned their homes, broke their bones and salted the earth in our path, when need be. But never against so small a settlement."

"No more than fifty people could have lived here," said Mälar. "Only the insane waste their time slaughtering so few. Why not simply defeat the warriors in battle and move on?"

"Because," whispered Halberd, "the witch taught all a lesson here."

Silence reigned.

"She is fearsome," said Usuthu.

He drew an arrow from his quiver.

"Shall I put this poor mad grandpa out of his misery?"

"No!" hissed Halberd, startling even himself with the force of his emotions. "We must not reveal our presence or our route. We must steel ourselves. Leave all your pity here. Let him suffer."

Mälar and Usuthu exchanged a glance. Usuthu put his arrow away.

"You are right, Shaman," said Mälar. "Fate is fate, and fate brought Grettir to this old man. You did not, my boy. Your role in the life of the witch was written before you were born. Do not take the lives of all in this village into your heart. You did not murder them."

Halberd said nothing. His blue eyes were as hard as glacial ice.

They returned to the trail and moved west. The old man's chant faded into the woods. In a few days he would be eaten by the snakes or the bears. If not, he would starve to death, and his body would be eaten by the snakes or the bears. When it happened Halberd and his crew would be leagues to the west.

Their wariness increased. A Skræling sentry could be waiting around the next bend.

The day passed but they came across no more villages. As light dwindled, they heard voices in the distance. The language was the coughing, clicking tongue of the Skrælings.

"Move with great caution," Mälar whispered. "We have stumbled atop a large village."

"Can you make it out?" Halberd asked. He lay on his stomach behind Mälar.

"Aye. It lies perhaps half a league up the trail, on the north side. We have good cover. Let us try to observe it and learn what we may."

Halberd looked back to Usuthu and held a finger to his lips. The Mongol nodded. He reached back and pulled Labrans to him by one arm. Usuthu clamped his hand over Labrans' mouth and drew his other hand across Labrans' throat. His arched eyebrows inquired if Labrans understood the message.

Labrans nodded. Usuthu let him go.

The four crawled off the path and into the underbrush. Thorns and thistles ripped their garments. Welts rose on their bodies. Mälar moved with remarkable soundlessness for a man of the sea. Delicately he parted each branch before him. With great care he brushed the ground for any twigs. When it was clear, he pulled himself a bit farther along.

The four men made a snake of their own, over twenty feet long. It took them many minutes to near the village. Light ended and a lingering purple twilight covered them. The Skræling sentries left their posts and walked to their fires for supper. The Northmen crawled quickly across the remaining feet to the camp.

They gazed down into the village. It, too, lay in a small depression below the level of the trail. Surrounding it was a thick wall of thorn bushes, through which the Northmen peered. The village hummed like a hive.

The Skrælings lived in longhouses made of bent saplings covered with bark. They resembled Northmen great-houses. They were long and narrow with curving roofs, like the hull of a boat turned upside-down. Several Skræling families seemed to live in each longhouse.

These were definitely the Eerhahkwoi. The men, tall and muscular, wore their hair in two long braids. In between these braids their hair stood in a thin line running from their foreheads to the back of their necks. They were all armed, even while eating in the village. They expected an attack.

Yet the village was calm. Children played, running about and screeching. Warriors spoke in muted tones to one another, exhibiting the dignity and quiet reserve which marked the savages of the Unknown World. After a meal of stew, served from a pot of crockery, the sentries left the village and returned to their posts.

The wind wafted the odor of stew to Halberd. It

smelled of deer and vegetables, thick and soothing and hot. His mouth filled with saliva. He lowered his head near the ground to empty his mouth.

Mälar bent his head to Halberd's ear.

"We are stuck fast, Shaman. Their guards are out. If we move we shall be found."

Halberd nodded. He looked to the Mongol.

Usuthu lowered his eyelids, mocking sleep. Halberd nodded again.

Mälar and Usuthu dropped their heads onto the dirt. They slept. Their years of hard fighting had taught them the gift of instant sleep and instant wakefulness. They took their rest where they could.

Halberd lay awake and watched the camp. The Skrælings were simply men, no more. Not demons, and not all that savage. They sat about and played with their children, they talked to their wives, they worked on their weapons.

These men need not be our enemies, thought Halberd. I wish them no harm.

His stiff back ached and he risked a glimpse at the stars. Half the night had passed. Halberd gently poked Usuthu in the side. The Mongol opened his eyes.

As he did, the crunching of someone walking through the thick brush sounded. A sentry moved toward them. He stopped a few feet away. Humming to himself, the sentry turned his back to the prone Northmen. A light splashing sounded in the bushes. Sighing contentedly when he was relieved, the Eerhahkwoi backed toward the Northmen. He trod squarely on Usuthu's arm.

Doubtless thinking the arm was a snake, the Skræling began to leap aside, raising his stone war club as he did. Usuthu snaked out one long arm. He snatched the Skræling by his dangling braid of hair and yanked him to the ground.

The Skræling hit between Usuthu and Halberd. Usuthu covered the man's nose and mouth with one huge hand. He pinched the Skræling's nose shut and held tight. With his other hand he punched the Skræling in the center of his throat. There was a faint crack.

The Eerhahkwoi's heels drummed in the brush. His back arched. He fell back, still. An unearthly stench rose from the dead man.

Any who live their lives in the woods develops senses like an animal. The stench of the poor man filled the air. As Halberd looked to Mälar, ready to give the command to flee, Labrans sat upright.

"Here we are, my brothers!" he screamed at the top of his lungs. "Come and find us, come and kill us, in the name of my mistress!"

He continued screaming, in an unknown, unrecognizable language. It could only be the language of the Eerhahkwoi. Usuthu clubbed him into unconsciousness and slung him over his shoulder.

They struggled through the thorns to their feet, seeking the best route. Usuthu, despite the weight and bulk of Labrans on his shoulder, leveled his bow and sent two arrows out. Two warriors sitting near the cook-fire flew backward, scattering flames and breaking cook-pots.

Mälar looked to the sky, searching for a star to

mark their path. Below, the village came awake with screams of women and shouts of men racing to their weapons. Skræling sentries crashed through the bushes, but in the darkness of night the Northmen could not see them.

"Usuthu," shouted Halberd, "did the man you strangled have a bow?"

Usuthu dropped Labrans to the ground and rummaged in the bushes. He held an Eerhahkwoi bow and quiver up for Halberd to see. The quiver, made of deer hide, was colorfully decorated with quills from a porcupine.

Usuthu held a finger to his lips. He was right. Shouting would give away their position in the darkness. Halberd swept his hand over the village. He wanted Usuthu to keep the warriors in the village pinned down while he and Mälar dealt with the sentries. Using Skræling arrows would not only confuse the savages, but also would not deplete Usuthu's own supply.

Again Usuthu nodded. He raised the bow and fired into the village. As he did, Halberd pushed Labrans along the ground until he lay just behind Usuthu. Again Mälar and Halberd stood back-to-back with Usuthu, Labrans lying between them.

Using the light of the fire, Usuthu wreaked terrible damage on the Skrælings. One burly warrior crawled from the opening in a longhouse, a stone-pointed lance raised high. Usuthu shot him through the throat and sent him hurling back into the longhouse. Three Eerhahkwoi in a group rushed past the fire, making for Usuthu's position. One hurled a lance at the Mongol and the other two drew stone-headed hatchets. All three sung a high, keening song.

The lance fell harmlessly short. Usuthu skewered all three before they had cleared the fire. Two older men emerged from a longhouse at the opposite end of the camp. One melted into the woods, bearing west. Usuthu shot the other before he could run from the clearing. The old man fell across the cooking fire and tumbled into the longhouse beside it. His flaming clothes ignited the longhouse. Women and children poured out of the burning structure. All of the women bore lances and shields.

Usuthu held his fire, searching for a male target.

The blaze from the burning longhouse lit up the night sky. The sentries spotted Halberd and shouted to their fellows, pointing their arms and trying to force their way through the unyielding brush.

One Skræling popped out of the dense thorns right in front of Mälar. The Eerhahkwoi registered surprise, but he raised his war club with admirable quickness. Mälar swung his axe horizontally, as if he was chopping down a tree. Halberd was amazed at the quickness and brutality of the blow. He had not seen the old man fight with such ferocity before.

Mälar felt fear. He fought for his life.

The ax bit deeply into the warrior. He fell to the ground, broken almost in half. Halberd held his position as Mälar braced one foot on the dead Skræling and worked the ax back and forth, trying to break it free.

Another warrior came out of the brush, following

91

the path the Northmen had forged. Halberd stepped past Mälar and lopped the man's arm from his shoulder with one stroke. Instead of going to his knees as Halberd expected, the warrior swung his other hand at Halberd's face. The hand clutched a brutal stone-headed mallet. Halberd had only time for a short chop at the swinging hand with his broadsword. The hand flew from the arm and disappeared into the brush. A gout of pulsing blood drenched Halberd. Mälar pulled the ax free finally, and spun toward Halberd. The Skræling stood rooted to the earth as he examined the spurting end of his arm.

Mälar raised the ax. Before he could strike, the Skræling fell over backward, dead. Usuthu never turned toward them. He trusted them. He knew he would not die while they protected his back.

The village was a pyre. Every longhouse now blazed, caught by sparks from the first. The bright light washed over the village and the woods around it. The Mongol and the Vikings stood clearly illuminated.

One old witchlike woman raised her arm and pointed at Usuthu. She screamed one word in their hideous tongue. All motion stopped. Across the village, on the rim surrounding it, the sentries fighting their way toward the explorers halted. Those below them trying to climb up also froze. Every one of the Skrælings stared at Usuthu. This was the first moment they could see him clearly. All gazed at him in awe and fear.

The flickering light reflected off Usuthu's smooth

black skin. The muscles bulged in his arms and neck. He stood well over seven feet tall, dripping sweat from his exertions, the Skræling bow in one hand, an arrow in the other. His slanted eyes gleamed fiercely. His drooping mustaches fell below his chin. The firelight showed his conical helmet and caused the huge shield he wore on his front and back to shine like suns.

None of the Skrælings moved.

"We must flee!" shouted Mälar. "Behold, their numbers are too great and our position is now marked. Let us make for the path."

"Flee?" Usuthu was thunderstruck. "I have never fled. When their men are dead we shall leave."

A Skræling arrow whizzed through the night and bounced off one of his shields. Another zipped by overheard.

"My brother," cried Halberd, "we have a quest. That is the source of our honor. We must subvert all to its conclusion. Come!"

Halberd pulled Usuthu's arm. A flight of arrows, perhaps ten or more, came out of the village. Halberd and Usuthu ducked and the arrows passed overhead. Usuthu returned fire. A wail of pain sounded over the crackling of the fires.

Usuthu slid his bow over his shoulder and handed the Skræling bow and quiver to Halberd. Usuthu slung Labrans over his opposite shoulder. He drew his curved bronze sword from his scabbard and led the way down the path. Halberd followed and Mälar formed the rear guard.

They plunged through the thick brush, Usuthu

slashing a path with his sword. When they reached
the main path once more, a Skræling leapt in front
of them. His hide clothes were burned and torn. A
wild light showed in his eye. He hefted his lance
and stepped near Usuthu.

Usuthu raised his sword overhead with both
hands. Labrans fell off his shoulder unnoticed. With
a wild grunt Usuthu swung the blade. It took the
Skræling on the right shoulder, swept through the
Eerhahkwoi and burst out again at his waist on the
left-hand side. The Skræling simply exploded, his
body torn in two clean halves. The Skræling's legs
stood upright for an instant. The upper body flipped
in the air. As it struck the rocky ground headfirst,
the legs crumpled.

Halberd stopped. The amazing force of the blow
stupefied him. It was the strongest thrust he had
ever seen any mortal make with any weapon. Around
the village the shouting of battle cries and the singing of songs stopped. All stared at the Mongol, who
stared down at the village defiantly. Those with
bows lowered them. Those moving forward with
lances or clubs or hatchets halted.

"I couldn't do that with this mighty ax," said
Mälar, in a small, stunned voice.

"Nor," Halberd answered, "could I."

Usuthu turned to face the village. He raised his
sword over his head with one hand and held the
other hand aloft in a clenched fist. He bared his
teeth at the village and screamed a long, wordless
shout. It was the cry of a victorious animal.

The Skrælings obviously believed him to be the

demon of Grettir's warning. No mortal could slice a man in twain with one blow of a sword.

"Let them worship you no longer!" screamed Mälar. "Seize the advantage and run. Run for all our lives!"

Usuthu looked at him without comprehension. The blood lust had driven him into another realm.

"Pick up Labrans and run, you great oaf!" said Mälar.

He shoved the Mongol in the chest.

Halberd took Usuthu by the arm. A Skræling arrow cut past them.

"Let us go, my brother," Halberd said calmly. "We are not welcome here and we have many leagues to travel."

Clumsily, as if numb, Usuthu lifted Labrans to his shoulder. Mälar fled west on the path. They followed him. Behind them, women threw dirt on the flames.

They ran in the classic warrior's trot until daybreak. Dawn brought thickening clouds and the promise of torrential spring rain. They passed no more villages. The ground had become higher and higher, yet they could see the sea no more. Some time in the night they had left it behind.

Gasping for breath, they knelt on the path. Labrans awakened and looked from face to face.

"Where are we, my brothers?" he asked.

"Try no more treachery, my poor enchanted fool," said Mälar. "We know of your mistress and you live only by the forbearance of your blood relative."

Labrans looked Halberd in the eye. He smiled

with sincerity and brotherly love. Halberd was touched to his heart. But only for a moment.

A chill swept over Halberd; Labrans had never smiled like that in his life, particularly not at Halberd. Halberd leaned closer and gazed back into his brother's guileless gaze. There, deep in Labrans' pupils, laughing with glee, was the face of Grettir. Halberd could see her clearly. He looked away. Perhaps Mälar was right. Perhaps his brother was lost, and Halberd struggled only to keep alive the shell.

"Tell me, brother," Halberd said, "how you gained your knowledge of the language of the Eerhahkwoi."

"I know it not," Labrans replied. His eyes were bright and he smiled like a child. "But I will try to learn it if that might aid you."

"This latest curse," said Halberd, "is also the cruelest; Labrans will seem not cursed at all. Say nothing in his presence that might aid the witch."

Labrans looked shocked and hurt. He lowered his head to the ground.

"But," Halberd continued, "if he is cursed, and part of that curse is understanding the Skræling tongue, then he will translate for me or I shall slay him where he stands."

"My brother," said Labrans, "I am not cursed. I serve at your side with pleasure."

"If you are not cursed," said Mälar pitilessly, "then you may run. Set the pace westward."

"We must rest" said Labrans. "Rest and eat."

"Labrans," said Halberd sharply, "we shall not eat here. We shall not rest. We shall not wait for the Eerhahkwoi to mourn their dead, subdue their fires, sharpen their weapons and gather their rations. We shall not wait for them to track us and we shall not wait for them to split our skulls. We shall run. You may lead the way."

"Now, go," said Usuthu, giving Labrans a shove. "Lead us."

Labrans set off down the path in a determined trot. The others gave him a start of several yards. They spoke quietly among themselves as they moved down the trail.

"Perhaps the witch has erred," Halberd said. "If I can dominate him with a spell of my own he may yet be our translator."

"Keep thinking that, Shaman," snorted Mälar. "The witch wants you to believe it so you will keep him a bit longer. He will not serve us. He serves only her."

They trotted another league in silence.

"How long do we travel at this pace?" asked Usuthu. "Never have I covered so much ground on foot."

"You are not tired, Usuthu?" Halberd asked. He had never seen Usuthu show any sign of physical weakness.

"No, I am merely bored. The land around me moves by much too slowly."

"Is this a new experience for you?" Halberd asked the question in a mild state of surprise; every warrior had run a few days at some point in his life. It was unavoidable.

"Yes," the Mongol grunted.

"Has a horse never died under you?" replied
Mälar.

"Never. Our ponies were tougher than almost
any man who rode them. They were bred to hard-
ship. They might live only ten years, but in that
time never rest one day. If a pony was slain in
battle another Mongol was always near. Any man
who walked home was regarded as a fool."

"You," said Halberd, "are a lucky man."

"I," said Mälar, without losing a step, "have seen
armies of spear-wielding bandits who serve the traders on the Inland Sea run at twice this pace for a
day and a night without stopping. They were of your
color, Usuthu, though they resembled you in no
other way, except height."

"Perhaps," said Mongol, "they were men of my
mother's tribe. She loved to run across the Great
Steppes. She disliked horses."

"Mälar," said Halberd, "'how could you have seen
these men run for a day and a night?"

"Simple, Shaman. I ran at their side."

"What," said Halberd, "is that?"

The daylight was fading. It was difficult to make
out what lay on the path. Whatever it was, Labrans
had run right past it. They stepped nearer. It was a
recently slain deer. Blood ran from huge gashes in
its side. The deer was large, with a great, spreading
rack of shiny brown antlers.

The deer's eyes were barely glazed. Minutes earlier it had lived.

Labrans came racing back down the path. His

eyes were wild with fright. His terror was instantly convincing. All raised their weapons.

"Bear!" screamed Labrans.

He ran past them. Mälar grabbed him as he went by and held him fast.

"Where?"

"Not half a league and running down the path. She scented me. Her fangs drip blood. I believe I disturbed her at a kill. She is larger than any bear in the Known World."

"This is her deer, her dinner," spat Mälar. "She will not be pleased to see us."

Usuthu nocked an arrow. Halberd fitted one into the Skræling bow. Perhaps two ship-lengths away, the path curved. They could not see around the bend. They heard the bear before she reached the curve. She roared deep in her throat. Her growls shook the trees.

She appeared at the bend. Labrans was not lying. She was larger than the Great Bears of the forest of the Short Ugly People Who Fornicate With Bears. She towered over Usuthu by her head and shoulders. She weighed more than all of them put together. Her claws were foot-long razors. Her huge fangs dripped blood.

"Oh Great Bear," called Usuthu, "forgive me. I have no quarrel with you or your spirit, but I will not be eaten."

He sighted carefully and let fly.

The bear raised her giant paws. She flicked one paw with the blurring speed of a hawk. With no apparent effort she swatted the arrow from the sky.

It broke against her paw and fell, in pieces, to the path.

There was a horrible moment as comprehension sank in.

The bear had knocked an arrow from the sky. An arrow fired by Usuthu.

It could not have happened.

Yet it did.

Usuthu recovered first.

"Run," he said.

He turned and raced toward the nearest tree. The branches were far above his head. Drawing his dagger as he turned, Usuthu took one huge step and jumped up the tree as far as he could. As he smashed into the rough trunk, he drove his dagger deep into the wood. Hanging from the knife with both hands, he turned and looked at the three below him.

"Climb!" he shouted.

Behind them, the bear roared again. Clods flew from her feet as she dug in. She made ready to charge.

For all his enchantment, Labrans had lost none of his desire to live. He placed one foot in the stirrup Mälar and Halberd made with their hands and reached up. He grabbed Usuthu's dangling feet and swiftly climbed up the Mongol's back. Standing on Usuthu's shoulders, Labrans stretched for the branches above. By hopping, he was able to grab the lowest one. He swung up and scrambled like a monkey high into the tree.

Mälar stood on Halberd's shoulders and grabbed the Mongol's feet. When he had a sure grip he looked down and nodded at Halberd. Halberd clutched the old man's feet and climbed up his back. Once he reached Usuthu's shoulders, he extended a hand for Mälar. Mälar swung past Halberd and vanished into the branches.

Halberd risked a look at the bear. She was halfway between the curve in the path and the tree. She was gathering speed. This bear moved faster than any horse.

Halberd climbed atop Usuthu's shoulders. He reached for the lowest branch and hung from it, his feet dangling in space. Usuthu grabbed Halberd's feet and pulled himself up the Viking's back. Halberd felt his hands tearing loose from the weight of the giant Mongol. He clenched his teeth and held on. Usuthu gained the branch and hauled Halberd up beside him with one huge hand.

The bear was at the foot of the tree. They were at least twenty feet above her, perhaps more. Halfway between the hunter and hunted, driven deeply into the tree, Usuthu's knife gleamed.

Usuthu pulled his bow off his shoulder and nocked an arrow.

The bear looked up expectantly. She roared with frustration. She stood on her hind legs and scraped the tree. Her claw marks reached almost to Usuthu's knife.

"What," asked Halberd, "if she can climb?"

"Then," replied Usuthu, sighting straight down into the bear's open mouth, "she will have no paws free for knocking down my arrows. Hence, she will die. Or at least be blinded."

The bear could not, it seemed, climb. She growled at her escaped dinner for some time, saliva frothing at her mouth. She tore all the bark from the trunk of the tree and big huge hunks from the wood. Eventually she left. It was by then full darkness.

As Halberd and Usuthu stood on their branch, stretching their legs, shouts in the Skræling tongue sounded. The shouts came from the east, whence the Vikings had fled the village of the Eerhahkwoi.

Over the shouting rose the full-throated roar of the she-bear. The shouting grew even louder. The roars of the bear mixed with the screams of the Skrælings. Both faded away, heading east. A fearsome battle seemed to be taking place. After some time the noise, including that of a satisfied bear eating her full, stopped. Peace returned to the forest.

Usuthu and Halberd climbed higher into the tree.

"Is that not the fastest creature you've ever seen?" exclaimed Mälar.

"Aye," said Halberd. "If the forests are filled with the likes of her, this shall be a difficult trek."

Usuthu started back down the tree.

"Where to, brother?" asked Mälar.

"If the she-bear dined tonight on Eerhahkwoi," Usuthu said, "then perhaps we may dine on deer."

Halberd followed the Mongol. They climbed down as they had climbed up. Usuthu hung from the branches and Halberd dangled from his feet. From there he dropped.

The deer lay on the path as before. The she-bear had had time to tear one huge bite out of the carcass before the Skræling had disturbed her. Halberd swiftly skinned and gutted the deer. Usuthu watched the path. Halberd wrapped the heart, liver and flanks into the bloody skin. He dragged the skin back to their tree.

"Give me the Skræling bow and arrows," Usuthu said.

Halberd took off the quiver and passed it to the Mongol. Usuthu restrung the bow and shook out every arrow. He paced back from the tree. Aiming carefully, as he always did, Usuthu fired an arrow into the tree about five feet off the ground. The next arrow struck the trunk about two feet above the first. And, so on.

Usuthu worked his way up the trunk until a rough ladder of arrows led to the lowest branch. They climbed without difficulty, retrieving Usuthu's dagger along the way. Each arrow that they climbed, Usuthu removed. Halberd tried to pull them from the tree, but they would not budge. Usuthu had fired them in to the depth of their guide-feathers.

The heart and liver were still warm.

"There is no shame in raw meat," said Mälar between the bloody mouthfuls. "No warrior worth the name has not dined as we do now."

"The power of a beast goes more quickly into your heart when you eat his," answered Usuthu. "This nourishment will last us for days."

Labrans refused food. He remained on the lower branches. A tangled triad of limbs formed his bed. Halberd leaned back against the trunk while Mälar scraped away at the inside of the deerskin with his knife.

"If only we had salt," he said, "then might I make a proper hide."

"If you are wishing on our behalf," said Halberd, "wish for ponies. We've weeks of walking awaiting us."

"Silence!" hissed Usuthu. He raised one hand.

They could hear leaves and twigs breaking below.

In the black of night, with deep storm clouds overhead as the first fat drops of chilling rain fell from the sky and ominous rumblings of thunder sounded in the distance, the Eerhahkwoi scouting party walked under the tree.

"These are formidable warriors," whispered Mälar. "We burn their village to the ground and a bear eats those we are unable to kill. Still, they come."

"This patrol might be from another village," Halberd said. "Pray for his storm to wash out our tracks. Give thanks also for this tree and its comforts. We'll not leave it soon."

As Halberd uttered these words, the storm broke. Lightning split the sky and thunder deafened them. The wind, which would not slacken for three days and nights, howled out of the north. There was no more conversation.

Thessah's Counsel

The sky lightened. The wind diminished. The clouds parted. Halberd raised his head. His memories had sustained him these three days and, now, through a fourth night.

Through all their time in the tree the storm raged without letup. Eerhahkwoi patrols searched the path below them night and day. Half of the deer the Northmen had cut into strips and hung for curing. The strips spoiled in the storm. No Skræling scout party had passed since the night before. There had been no food for two days.

They had to move.

Mälar stirred at Halberd's movement. He reached out and gently touched Usuthu's shoulder. The Mongol opened his eyes. He came fully awake. He scanned the sky.

"The sky breaks. We must travel."

"Leave the deerskin for our return trip," Mälar said. "Let the savages find it and see how we out-foxed them, the diligent fools."

"They will not rest," Halberd replied. "Doubtless their runners traveled west to warn other villages of our approach. We behaved precisely as Grettir told them we would. We slew their warriors and burnt their village. They will not rest. Nor shall we."

They awoke Labrans and reached the ground. Their muscles ached and their bones creaked.

"I have been wetter and stiffer," said Mälar. "I'm sure of it. But it seems I'm unable to remember when."

"We must find game," Usuthu said. "I will run ahead and kill the first living creature I see, be it bear, spider or even snake."

"Search not only for game, brother," said Halberd, "but for a cave as well."

"We must have movement," Mälar said, alarmed, "I cannot be cooped up again."

"I will learn the way of Hrungnir," Halberd said. "Tonight I dream and speak to my mother. She will know. I will be in a deep trance. My body must be guarded."

"How long a dream?" Usuthu asked.

"It may take one night, it may take three, I do not know. I know that we may travel no farther until I understand this sacred weapon."

"Very well, Shaman," said Mälar. "I'll hunt with Usuthu. I must stretch my aching legs."

The two hefted their weapons and trotted west. The forest swallowed them.

Halberd drew Hrungnir. He gently placed the point against Labrans' heart.

"Lie down, brother," Halberd said. "I cannot turn my back on you. I cannot guard you alone. I must bind you."

"Not your brother. Not me. You've taken my weapons. I am defenseless. Do not do me this final injustice."

"That is not your voice, Labrans. It is the voice of the witch. I do not hear it."

Halberd bound his brother's hands behind him and lifted him to his feet.

"Now we walk in safety," Halberd said.

"Do you not miss me a little?"

Halberd whirled. The voice was Grettir's. Its source was the mouth of his brother. Grettir's voice, soft and sweet, brought his loins awake.

"No, witch," he said.

Halberd prodded Labrans in front of him. They trotted down the path.

"Do you not remember the things we did together?" the witch asked. "Do you not remember my mouth upon you, and your fingers inside me? Can you not recall how I felt astride you? How our sweat merged? How my legs felt around you?"

"I remember my brother's broken back," Halberd answered. "I remember this knife driven into his spine. I remember the foul dwarf, Thund, leading my brave brother to Niflheim. That is all I can remember."

"You cannot forget what you feel for me."

"That is undoubtedly my curse. I will learn how to break the spell which you hold over my brother. Until then, I will not hear your words."

Halberd pushed Labans to the ground. He cut a strip from Labrans' cloak and gagged him tightly.

"I am sorry, Labrans," Halberd said. "Your mistress has left me little choice."

Nothing human showed in Labrans' eyes. They were glazed and dull. Halberd and Labrans set off west in a determined trot.

The ground grew hilly. They were well inland. The forest thinned and more trails appeared. Whenever a junction neared Halberd instinctively took the broadest and best packed trail leading northwest. He knew the trails might double back. He did not worry. He trusted that the large trails were main traffic paths.

Mälar and Usuthu marked each trail with a bit of cloth or a a slash cut into a tree trunk. The morning passed without incident. Halberd felt lean and strong. His breath came easily. He was fit and ready to fight. Though they had leagues to cover, Halberd felt no concern.

He was baffled by his own confidence. Their way was not going to be easy. Yet for the first time since Valdane had been slain, Halberd felt the wheel of fate turning to favor him. A long visit with his mother would restore him. Moreover, she knew more legends of the dark knowledge than any Skald in Northland.

Halberd felt no concern that Mälar and Usuthu had not yet halted. They were explorers. They would rather travel than stop, and their hunger would quiet once they started moving. As for Skrælings, Halberd would fight if need be, or flee.

Halberd stopped for a pull at one of his water-skins. His breath came easily. He undid Labrans' gag and offered him a drink. Labrans turned his head away.

In their village in Northland, Labrans drank mead. By the cask. He never walked if he could ride. He never hunted. He sat by his father's fire, did his father's accounts and dreamed of adventure. He seldom actually had adventures. He seldom went on expeditions with Valdane and Halberd. Perhaps he had been jealous of their closeness.

After Valdane had sailed to Vinland, Labrans trained with his weapons in earnest. A fair swords-man, he became a decent archer and a master of the lance. He remained fat and clumsy, though strong. Perhaps he intended to usurp command of the sec-ond Vinland voyage from Halberd. Perhaps he was finally ready to leave the farm. It was too late, in any case.

Since his enchantment, Labrans' body had al-tered. This morning he ran without a drink, without a rest, without a single stumble or misstep on the rocky path. With his hands tied behind him and his mouth gagged. Whatever Grettir had in store for Labrans, she treated him well. Perhaps, in his deep-est heart, Labrans had always yearned for grace. To keep him content as a slave Grettir had given it to him.

This new coordination would make him formida-ble in a fight. Halberd would keep all arms away from Labrans.

They kept moving. The trees were no longer evergreen. They had thick, waxy leaves and huge, broad trunks. Halberd passed much game: deer, elk, easily slain birds with rich white meat. The game animals ignored him. They strolled about the woods as if a man constituted no threat.

Usuthu was the hunter today, and when Usuthu found the meat he wanted, he would stop. Halberd didn't feel sufficient hungry to risk insulting Usuthu. Halberd would wait for the dinner that Usuthu chose.

They rounded a bend. Lying on the trail were four Skrælings. All were dead. All lacked heads. Just beyond them, hanging from a huge arrow, was an elk pinned to a tree trunk. All four hooves were off the ground. The elk had been gutted. His blood slowly dripped onto the path. He was not dead long enough for flies to gather. The same could be said for the Skrælings.

"Ho, Shaman!"

Halberd turned around. Mälar's call came from behind hm. When he turned, he saw no one. Halberd scanned the trees. The branches were too thick to see more than a few feet overhead.

"Shaman, blindfold your brother. Fill his ears."

Halberd took the gag from Labrans' mouth and covered his eyes. He tore new strips from Labrans' tunic and stuffed these into his ears.

"Look below the elk."

Halberd stared at the base of the tree. A bush beside the blood pool moved. Usuthu's head rose from below the ground. His shoulders were below ground level.

"By the gods!" Halberd said. "You were invisible. What have you found?"

"Our new dry home," he answered. "Come and see."

The usually taciturn Mongol grinned from ear to ear. Halberd crossed the trail and looked down. Usuthu stood in a narrow hole. It was barely wide enough for his shoulders. Beside the hole was a large, flat rock.

"Pass me your enslaved brother," Usuthu said. "There is only room enough for one at a time to pass through the entrance."

"Entrance to where?" Halberd asked. "And where is Mälar?"

"He stands watch in one of the trees. We found this place only moments ago. We slew the Skrælings when they startled my elk. Otherwise we'd have let them pass in peace. And ignorance."

Halberd guided the deaf, dumb and blind Labrans to the edge of the hole. Usuthu simply disappeared. Halberd could not see where he went.

Halberd sat Labrans on the edge of the hole. From there he lowered his brother by the shoulders until Labrans stood in the hole as Usuthu had stood. Labrans did not come up to the level of the ground. His head was more than a foot and a half below it.

Halberd leaned over the edge of the hole. At its base was another, wider opening perpendicular to the first hole. Usuthu's head popped out of this hole. He swung Labrans around and pulled him feet first into the second hole.

Halberd jumped in after him. He lay on his back

and stuck his legs into the hole. Usuthu pulled him in.

Halberd stood on a shelf at the roof of a huge cavern. Broken rocks formed a rough natural staircase to the bottom of the cave, which was several man-heights below. Light filtered in from many invisible holes. A softly bubbling stream gurgled against one wall of the cave. Several large rocks made natural sleeping platforms. Except for the area around the spring and its runoff, the cave was dry as a bone. There were no bats, no bear dung and no sign of human habitation; no ashes, no bones, no old cookfires.

"How have you found this miracle?"

"I hid behind the tree to slay the elk. When the first Skræling appeared I thought he was alone. I hefted the large rock to bash in his skull. Below it was the hole. I jumped in. As an archer's roost it was perfection. I could see and not be seen. No arrow could strike yet I could shoot with ease."

"But," said Halberd, "those Skrælings are beheaded. No arrow killed them."

"Yes," Usuthu said. "'As I drew down on them, Mälar raced along the path like a wild animal. He slew the first two with one blow of your axe. All this bloodshed and battle at close quarters has made him a young man again. He relishes man-to-man combat. I fear he will never fire a bow again."

"Mälar," said Halberd, dumbfounded, "killed all four, unaided?"

"Perhaps I held the last one with the point of my

dagger in his back, the better to steady him up for the lethal blow. But all the glory should go to the old man."

"Then how did you discover this cavern?"

"When I braced my foot to fire my bow, I kicked rocks through the entry hole. After the elk was slain I investigated farther."

"How," said Halberd, weary as a teaching Skald with a roomful of five-year-olds, "did the elk come to be pinned to the tree? I've never seen an animal of that size hanging in space."

"I believe that is due to the extremely close range from which I fired my arrow."

"How close?"

"Fewer feet than you are tall, my brother."

"The elk did not bolt while Mälar chopped off the heads of the Skrælings a few steps down the path?"

"The animals here do not fear man. In fact, they fear nothing. We will eat well."

"I suppose we will."

"Well," Usuthu said, "I cannot stay here and tell you tales of our adventures when so much remains to be done. You stay here and tend to your brother. I will skin the elk. Mälar gathered firewood enough for days. When you hear it crash into the bottom of the first hole, gather it in."

Halberd bound Labrans' hands in front of him. Then he lay his brother on a shelf of rock and placed a water skin in his hands. Halberd struck a few twigs into flame with his flint and watched the

smoke carefully. A solid updraft drew it to the roof
of the cave, where it dissipated through twenty
different holes. No one could track this cave by the
smoke. They might smell it, but they would never
find it.

Large bundles of firewood crashed onto the floor
of the first hole. Halberd poked his head out of the
lower hole and there, right before his jaw, as if his
head were resting on a table, was the firewood. He
carried it below and built a large, orderly stack,
near the place he had chosen for the cook-fire.

Another, more solid, thump announced that the
elk had arrived. Halberd once more reached out
and gathered in the bloody hindquarters. Each thump
returned him to the hole until the entire elk rested
inside, including the skin.

Halberd was slicing thin strips for curing at the
fire when Mälar dropped through the entry. Over
their heads sounded a horrible scraping noise.

Halberd reached for his sword. Mälar waved him
off.

"Usuthu drags the covering stone over the upper
hole," he said. "Two bears might move it, or one
Giant, but certainly no other mortal."

Usuthu slid through the upper opening. He went
to the firewood stack and began the cook-fire. Mälar
filled the water skins from the spring. Halberd
untied Labrans and removed his blindfold and gag.

"Can you hear me, brother?" Halberd asked.

"I hear you."

"If you move to the opening of this cave, or make
any loud noises during my dream, one of these men

will kill you. Then you will be of no use to your mistress."

"I understand, though I have no mistress. Where are we?"

Halberd looked to Mälar.

"Ask the navigator," he said.

"We have run for over one week while you remained in a trance," Mälar said. "We crossed mighty rivers and mountain ranges such as we have never seen. I calculate that we shall reach the Thundering Falls in less than three days."

Halberd and Usuthu turned away so Labrans could not see their faces. Both made themselves busy with chores. The old dog had not yet lost his cunning.

"And this cave?" said Labrans.

"It is high in the side of a mountain covered with trees to the very crest. A huge cliff covers half the mountain. We camp on the side opposite this cliff."

"Why do we rest?"

"We have food and shelter. We may have neither for some time."

Labrans turned away, nodding. He smiled his soft, secret smile once more.

Mälar joined Halberd and Usuthu at the fire.

"However it might grieve your heart," Mälar said, "I fear you must bind your brother before you dream. If the witch discovers you are dreaming she may attack you in that world."

"Can she detect us here, in this rock?" Usuthu asked.

"I do not know," Halberd said. "Mälar may have confused her. If she thinks we are near the falls she may turn her attention to traveling."

"Not, perhaps," Mälar said, "a bad idea. When will we do the same?"

"You must be patient," Halberd said. "Though I cannot explain it, I feel we are in no hurry. I am convinced, against all evidence, that we shall make the falls before the witch. I have several dreams to dream, and I will need time."

"You," Mälar said, "have the powers of prophecy, not I. Have faith in your instincts. Believe in your gifts and I shall do the same."

Mälar went across the cave. Over Labrans' loud protests he again blindfolded the bewitched Northman

"Usuthu," Halberd said, "why did you chop that Skræling in twain? Why did you snatch that elk from his feet with an arrow? These are spectacular deeds, but they are unlike you. They are . . ." Halberd paused to think, ". . . excessive."

Usuthu leaned close to Halberd. His teeth were clenched. Usuthu's words emerged with diffculty.

"You cannot know," he said, "how it pains me to flee. I fear cowardice is overtaking my nature."

"How can you say this? You fight like no mortal on this Earth."

"I ran from the Skrælings. I also ran from the bear. Several times on the path today I hid behind bushes to allow a large force of warriors to pass. I killed none of them."

"That bear knocked down an arrow in mid-flight. It was invincible."

"When my arrow proved useless I should have drawn my sword. If the she-bear killed me, so be it. Likewise the Skrælings."

Halberd spoke with great care.

"Usuthu, if you do not flee, if you do not hide, if you are killed, then you betray our oath of brotherhood. If I allow you to die in battle then I have betrayed mine. We have a quest. We must fulfill it."

"Before my oath to you, I swore one to Bahaab Dahaabs—to fight as a Mongol fights. To fear nothing and accept death happily."

"Can you deny this urge to die? Can you serve your two brothers here in this Unknown World, and remain alive as their protector?"

"I cannot say. I will try. But know this, when a chance to spill blood arrives, I will spill every drop I may. Do not ask me to run from a fight once the fight is joined."

"I shall not. Will you guard me as I dream?"

"Of course, my brother."

They clasped forearms in the grip of friendship.

Malar brought charred elk from the fire.

"Eat hearty, Shaman. You will need this where you are going."

"And you, old man," Halberd said, "you slice the heads from warriors. You take my ax, do not return it. You look for combat."

"I am rejuvenated, Halberd. Too many years have I been at sea, standing at the tiller and calling commands while others swung their swords. I've forgotten the exalted feel of a blade biting into flesh. I am a Northman. Now I am remembering how to be a warrior."

Halbert stuffed himself with elk. Malar and Usuthu pressed him to eat the heart, the source of the elk's power. Halberd was careful to eat only a third. Protesting fullness, he refused more. Malar and Usuthu consumed the rest. Labrans would not eat.

Halberd lay on a shelf of rock. He slid under an overhang. He could not be seen. If Labrans was untied they would tell him that Halberd was out on a hunt.

Halberd held Hrungnir tightly in one hand. In the other he gripped his broadsword. Ishlanawanda had told him that the Jewel of Kyrwyn-Coyne, which rested in a filigree of silver in the butt of his sword, and the stone knife were linked. He wanted both with him in his dream.

"Do not be too bored," he said to Usuthu.

"Fear not, brother. I will protect you. Now sleep. Halberd slept.

Halberd moves through a world of mist. Black craggy mountains loom in front of him. He is not walking, but not flying. He skims the ground. His legs move, but his feet make no contact with the earth. Halberd makes a walking motion but he travels faster than any man afoot. Than any man on horseback. Than any hawk, any eagle, any mortal thing.

Never before has Halberd been forced to navigate in a dream. He dreams of Ishlanawanda's village and he is there. Never has he attempted the ultimate feat of Dream Magic: to appear in the dream of someone else. He does not attempt it now. He seeks only to send his Dream Self back to the village of his birth.

It seems that to travel this great distance, even in a dream, requires time. As Halberd whisks through this Dream landscape he concentrates on the face of his mother, Thessah.

Thessah is a gifted Skald, a spiritual leader, a teller of tales, a Keeper of Myths, a Healing Woman. She understands the herbs that defeat illness; she communes with the spirits of the dead; she is the living repository of all the ancient knowledge of their village, and, remarkably, other villages as well. Few worthy candidates appear in any lifetime, and Thessah's gifts are too powerful to ignore. Breaking convention, other aged Skalds came from every corner of Vinland to teach their secret ways and unknown spells to Thessah. So what if their village has lost the exclusive right to this knowledge? At least it will be passed on to someone who understands its significance.

Thessah, along with others, has misread Grettir. Thessah saw that Grettir has powers. She taught Grettir much, but Grettir misused the power of this knowledge. Thessah has no idea how powerful Grettir has become. Nor does Thessah know that she has to chose another successor, another young woman to learn the knowledge of the Skalds. Grettir will not be coming home.

Halberd puts his faith in Thessah's sensitivity and her alertness to the Spirit World. After all, it was from her that Halberd inherited his gifts in such matters. She would know that he cast his spirit out in search of her. She would wait. She would be receptive. She would guide him to her, just as he sought her out.

Halberd had no sense of time. The mountains give way to endless forests. The trees are not green; their leaves are black. Fog swirls about the tree-tops. Halberd races atop the fog. When the forest is broken by streams or rivers, the water is glistening black. Strange howls and growls climb out of the forest. One may die in a dream as easily as in life, and this black forest offers little comfort. What creatures roam there, Halberd dares not guess.

Walking through those woods would guarantee adventure, and most likely death.

After a time the forest vanishes and ocean appears. This water is not green or blue but deep, unfathomable black. No waves break its surface. No ships sail. The endless sea is calm and unmarked. It is untroubled as a vast lake at twilight, but Halberd knows it is ocean.

Here there is no fog. Halberd dances over this water, watching the surface for some hellish creature sent by Grettir, or even Hel, Goddess of the Under-world. Immortals may go where they please, Dream World or Waking.

Halberd sails and sails over the ocean. Dim shoreline appears on the horizon. The sun rises as Halberd nears the shore. The sunrise is not black, but red and gold and spectacular. The shoreline is green and blue. Deep fjords split the mountains. Snow-capped peaks explode out of the ocean. Rich, verdant forest reach to the water's edge. Dragon-ships ply the sounds that lead from the sea inland.

Halberd reaches his true home. He returns to Vinland.

The next instant he sits by the fire in his father's house. It is early spring. Snow still rests under the eaves on the north side of the stone great-house. The house is chilled, and the fire provides the only warmth. Halberd cannot feel the cold or the fire. His body is not there. Only his Dream Self. In the Dream World, Halberd may hear, speak and observe. That is all. He may not touch.

Thessah looks up from the cast of runes she makes on the floor.

The oddly marked bones scattered on the floor by her toss cease moving and clacking as Halberd enters the house. Thessah gasps. Tears spurt from her eyes.

"Tell me quickly," she says through her tears, "are you dead? Do I speak to a ghost?"

Halberd fights back the tears that well inside him.

"No, Mother," he says. "I have sent myself to your side in a dream. I must have your counsel."

Thessah shakes her head. In her eyes are love, a certain awe and even a bit of fear.

"How have you gained such knowledge? This is

the stuff of legend. No Skald in this land knows of one who may do what you have done."

"How these powers come to me I do not know. My ignorance far exceeds my pitiful knowledge. I urgently need your help."

"Aye. The runes told me my son would be coming home soon. The message was ambiguous. I did not know which son I would see. I feared I might see your ghost."

Halberd looks carefully at his mother. She appears well. Her hair holds a tiny bit more gray.

"How fare you, Mother, since the death of my brother, Valdane?"

"My sons are warriors, Halberd. Adventurers. True Northmen. How many men live to die at home by the hearth? Your father seldom roams because I made him swear that he would not die except by my side. Why do you think he never traveled without the company of his sons? He knew you would protect him.

"I made him swear because I expected my sons to die in distant lands or to drown in distant seas. It is a Viking's life. How could I change it?"

"Father told you of Valdane's death?"

Thessah nods her head.

"And of Mahvreeds?"

She shakes her head this time, not daring to speak.

"He fought bravely," Halberd says, "defending his brother and his men against Grettir and two dwarves from Niflheim. He had no chance."

"And Labrans," Thessah asks, "my good-for-nothing layabout son? Is he also dead? Runes and spells speak to me in contradictions when I inquire of him."

"Grettir enslaves him with a spell. We guard him closely, but I know he will try to kill me. He waits only for the moment."

"Halberd!" Thessah speaks sharply, a mother to an infant son, "have you forgotten all I taught you? Any man who falls prey to a spell allows himself to be enslaved. Labrans was seduced by Grettir. If he was not drawn to her dark powers, then he would not now be enslaved! If he tries to kill you, then you must bury the sentimental foolishness that has always marred your judgment."

"How can you speak thus of your son?"

"I would tell him the same of you. Save my son if you can. If you cannot, why should two of my sons die?"

Halberd's heart breaks. The deed he could never confess to his dead brother, Valdane, Halberd must confess to his mother.

"But, Mother," Halberd cries, "I am as seduced as Labrans. On the day of Valdane's wedding, on the day they sailed for Vinland, I made love with Grettir. I am the lover of my brother's wife. Her witchcraft is my doing! I cursed her with our infidelity. Our act triggered the dark forces inside her."

Thessah smiles at her son. She shakes her head ruefully.

"This is indeed a tragedy," she says quietly, in a voice full of love, "but it is not your fault.

"Everyone in this village knew of your lust for her, and hers for you. Many times did Valdane discuss this problem with your father and I. You would take no other woman as a lover and she was full of urges she could not control. After much discussion we agreed that Valdane might turn his back. With her love of deceit, Grettir would doubtless pursue you. If you became lovers, fine. If not, again that was fine."

"But this is forbidden. How could you sanction it?"

"We hoped that she might teach you of the physical world, and that your sweetness might temper her hard ambition. Apparently it did not."

"Valdane knew?" he asks.

"Yes. When you two remained absent from the wedding for so long, we all surmised. Valdane bore you no jealousy. He was glad."

"What, then, caused this metamorphosis in Grettir?"

"The change, I think, was slight. She was always a witch. I helped her gain her power," Thessah says with great bitterness. "The tragedy is how much I misjudged her. It is the greatest mistake of my life as a Skald. And look at the price it has cost!

"She seemed a sweet girl with a great thirst for Dark Knowledge, at first. The more she learned, the harder and more ambitious she became. Because, I, too, was blinded by her charm I assumed this new hardness was necessary. After all, she was sailing to Vinland. Is there a harsher place in the

Known World? She needed strength for such a journey.

"The lessons I taught her she put to evil purpose. She made contact, I do not know how, with the forces of the Giants and Dwarves. She visited me in my Dreams, mocking me and telling me of Valdane's death. I hate her bitterly.

"She betrayed the love I gave her, she betrayed your love and Valdane's. When you find her, show her no mercy."

Thessah's eyes gleam. Her teeth show brightly. Her fists clench.

"She lied to me." Thessah's voice is the merest, harshest whisper. "She stole the lives of three of my sons. Do not let her steal yours. Take your vengeance in the name of this family. Take vengeance in the name of all the Skalds of this land, those whose knowledge Grettir has used to foul ends. Those whose sacred knowledge she has betrayed. Take vengeance for me."

"Mother, I shall take this vengeance. But to achieve it I need your aid."

"How may I help you?" Her voice is calm. She gently places a few sticks in the fire. Her rage has swept through her. In its place is an icy calm. She demonstrates for the first time the depth of her power as a Skald.

"Grettir slew Valdane with this." Halberd pulls Hrungnir from its holster. "I must know how best to wield it. Whence it comes. How it may aid me and how it may harm me."

Thessah says nothing. She stares at the stone

knife for a long time. She turns her gaze to the fire. It snaps as the flames lick the new logs. Thessah sighs. When she again raises her face to Halberd, she has visibly aged. Her mouth is set in a hard line. Her eyes are like two blue stones.

"The prophecy is true," she says. Again she looks away with a sigh.

Halberd waits. He says nothing.

"You were born," Thessah speaks softly, "the seventh son of a seventh son. The birthing Skald prophesied great spiritual powers for you, my son. Today you appear before me bearing a weapon no mortal has ever touched, in all the years of legend. Never touched! Yet you carry it in a pouch and wave it around like a stick of firewood. You are a powerful man, my son. I have yearned for great knowledge. I know much.

"But you, my son, you know too much. Your gift may well be a curse. You are too powerful. Pray that your sweet side never loses its strength. Pray that somehow you find love in the Unknown World. If you do not, you could easily become a demon like Grettir. You will be sorely tempted by evil. You will even be tempted by Grettir. Her sexual power is strong. Resist it. If you join Grettir you will command unearthly powers."

"Mother," Halberd says excitedly, "I have found my love! She lives in the Dream World; she is young and powerful herself. Her beauty is great."

"Tell me no more," Thessah interrupts. "Only you, Halberd, would choose as a lover a woman from the Dream World. Do you suppose this has ever happened? Ever? It has not. You blaze new paths. How on this earth, in this world, can I help you?"

"Tell me of Hrungnir, its history and power. How might I use it?"

Thessah absentmindedly gathers her runes from the floor. Clacking them in her hands, turning them over and over, she gazes into the fire and speaks: "None but the Skalds ever mention this knife. It belongs to the Immortals. I have never told you tales of it. It comes, indirectly, from Loki the Trickster himself.

"As you know, Loki had two children by the Giantess, Cathub. Their issue is horrible to describe. One is his daughter, Hel, the half-dead, half-living creature who rules Niflheim. Odin cast her from Aesir and into the Underworld because all the Gods feared her. Further, she was so foul to gaze upon that she upset the Gods at their meals.

"Loki's other child is Svipdag, the Wolf. The Gods feared this giant wolf and tricked him into being bound. They trussed him up and hurled him deep underground. There the Gods pinned his jaws open with a sword stuck deep into the roof of his mouth. The wolf was manacled to a rock and left for eternity.

"This wolf has never ceased to rage against his bonds. He struggles and turns and grunts. When the Earth itself rises up and cracks, or the very ground shakes, it is because Svipdag has shuddered so.

"From the immortal wolf's mouth, which is stuck open, drool constantly pours. Thick, rich, white curds of spittle. Often, when the ground breaks open or mountains spew flame, it is Svipdag's drool that runs from the fissures or down the mountainside. It is red-hot, or even white-hot. When it cools, it is hard but full of air, like the stone knife.

"This drool first ran down through many underground passages and into Niflheim, where Hel identified it. She knew it ran from the mouth of her trapped brother. She could not violate the will of the Gods and save Svipdag. She hated the Gods for stealing from her brother, his freedom. But, just as she had power, she knew her that poor brother had powers as well.

"She schemed and schemed. Hel is potent, but she is not smart. While she schemed, others acted. The Giants also observed what the gods did to Svipdag. They were filled with outrage. After all, Svipdag's mother was one of them. One such Giant, Ragnarok, traveled at great peril down into the caverns that lie between Earth and Niflheim. In such a cavern, Ragnarok found Svipdag.

"The drool poured from the wolf's mouth. It steamed. Ragnarok was in grave danger. The Gods would punish him horribly if they caught him in the cavern. Hel would kill him. Even Svipdag would have killed the Giant, if he could have.

"Ragnarok made no move to free the wolf. He knew that the tether the Gods had made was unbreakable. Instead, he put his huge hands inside the drooling jaws of the wolf. Svipdag went berserk trying to bite the Giant. The drool poured out even more fiercely, even hotter.

"The Giant caught this drool in his hands. Though his flesh burned and smoke rose from his palms he did not let go of it. Yet it was so hot he could not hold as much as he wanted. He was forced to take only a tiny bit. He rolled it between his hands until he had formed a long cone. Then he twisted it into a point and scooped the small hole you see in the top.

"He ran back to Midgard bearing the rapidly cooling drool in his burned and charred palms. The speed of his running made it cool faster. When it had cooled it formed into the shape you now hold, the shape of an elongated pyramid.

"This pyramid is strong. It may kill Immortals. It may enchant. It may transport its owner to any place a God may go, since it contains blood from Loki's offspring, any place a Giant may go, since the wolf's mother was a Giant and anywhere in any world that any Immortal may go.

"All this is legend. Skalds have known this tale since the time of my grandmother's grandmother. What I do not know, what I cannot understand, is how you came to possess it."

"I think I understand," Halberd says. "I slew the Dwarf, Thund, with this knife. When I cut open the hump in his back, three Giants escaped therefrom, or at least the ghosts of three Giants. Their names were Urd, Ull and Ragnarok.

"I believe that somehow Thund slew Ragnarok

and took from him Hrungnir. He then delivered this knife to his mistress, Hel. Hel loaned Grettir the knife so that Grettir might slay Valdane."

"Why would Hel strike a bargain with any mortal?" Thessah wonders aloud.

"Because, Mother, Valdane was no ordinary mortal, as you know. He was a great warrior, a fighting man of legend. Upon his death, he was destined for Aasgard, there to spend eternity fighting and brawling with his fellow Northman heroes.

"Hel has use for such a hero. She has many battles of her own to fight. Yet all the finest warriors are in Aasgard. Only the evil ones, the cowards and the dregs end up in Niflheim. If Grettir could slay Valdane with Hrungnir, she could then enslave him and consign his soul to Hel. Thence did Hel give Grettir loan of Hrungnir.

"Grettir slew Valdane with the stone knife. She left it in his back to enslave him until Thund the Dwarf, arrived to seize my poor brother.

"She cast a spell over Hrungnir: Only a true guardian of Valdane's soul could pull the knife from Valdane's back. Since Grettir consigned Valdane's soul to Thund the Dwarf, Grettir meant that only Thund could remove the knife.

"Grettir and Thund had conspired together against Hel. Thund would give the knife to Grettir and then transport Valdane to Niflheim. Grettir hoped that Hel would be so pleased to receive Valdane that Hel would forget about the knife.

"But I arrived. I, and only I, am the true guardian of Valdane's soul. I pulled the knife from my brother and used it to slay Thund. I could not prevent my brother from being taken to Niflheim, but I gained this great knife. I will use it one day to free my brother from Hel's grip."

Thessah shakes her head gravely. "Do not make these vows, my son. If you can free Valdane, you shall. Do not torment yourself if you cannot."

"Tell me more of Hrungnir's power," Halberd says, ignoring her warning.

"It may freeze the passage of time. I know that the Jewel of Kyrwyn-Coyne and Hrungnir are destined in legend to be combined, but how and to what end I do not know."

"How may I travel in the Dream World without it, and still be protected by it?"

"Again, this is a question I may not answer. These powers are well hidden, my son, but they are also obvious. Study Hrungnir and study the jewel as well. Study their physical makeup. The answer cannot be so well concealed. Remember always, the Gods are immortal, the Gods each possess a specific power, but the Gods are no smarter nor purer than we pathetic mortals. Any puzzle they might unlock, we might unlock as well."

"Mother, my heart is restored at the sight of you and all you have told me. I love you dearly."

"And I you, Halberd."

"Now I know why I feel no urgency in my pursuit of Grettir. Before I chase her another step, I will travel to Niflheim. I will free my brother from the clutches of Hel."

"Hel is the daughter of Loki. She is not bright, but she is devious. Give her no time to think. Spend only a short while in Niflheim. Never turn your back to her or make any promise or bargain. She may snatch you from the living world if she desires. Any who visit Niflheim sacrifices the right of return. Your soul would be in her hands."

"No, Mother. I have power in my hands, in this knife. When next I return I will bring to you my brother's ghost."

"Never!" Thessah shouts. "Death is death. I know too much of its undoing to have it undone. Valdane is dead. He is lost to me. I have communed with ghosts. I have spoken to the dead. I have raised ghosts for families who could not bear to be without the one who had died. Every family was happier before they met the ghost.

"A special bond binds you and Valdane. You have spoken to his ghost. For you it is a different matter. For me it is only the heartbreak of his death all over again. Bring yourself to me when you may, but never bring any who do not live."

"May I bring into your dreams the woman whom I love?"

"Do not invade my dreams, Halberd. Grettir has tried. I have set traps for any who venture into my head while I slumber. I have called upon the strongest spells I know. Come to me only when I am awake."

"I shall, dear mother. Will I see my father today?"

"No. He sits in his judge's chair. He will not be home until tomorrow."

"Tell him all my news. Give him my love."

Halberd reaches for his mother. His hands pass through her. He looks at the floor, embarrassed at his clumsiness. She smiles at him, a smile of great strength and formidable love.

He leaves the house and again races across the black, black ocean, Hrungnir clasped tightly in his hand. The ocean gives way to forest, the forest to mountains. The black, fog-shrouded mountains in turn give way to the cave.

Halberd awakes.

A Cold Day in Niflheim

Halberd opened his eyes. Mälar's back rested on Halberd's sleeping shelf. Mälar dozed, his head on his knees. Across the cave, Labrans crept silently toward Mälar. Halberd could not see Usuthu. Labrans drew nearer. His hands reached out like claws.

"Enough!" cried Halberd.

Labrans jumped at Mälar. Mälar came awake. Labrans landed on the old sailor, his hands wrapped around Mälar's throat. Halberd rolled out of his furs. He drove the point of Hrungnir just deep enough into Labrans' back to bring a drop of blood.

"By the power of Hrungnir," Halberd called, "I command you to remember your vow!"

Labrans fell back onto the cave floor. His mouth hung open. His eyes filled with confusion. Mälar raised the axe to strike. Halberd seized him by one wrist.

"Hold!" Halberd whispered.

In a child's voice, a quaking, frightened voice, Labrans asked: "What vow?"

"The vow you swore on Vinland," Halberd thundered. "To serve as my bodyguard and protect me from any harm."

"I . . . I . . ." Labrans fought for breath. "I cannot," he said in his normal voice, a voice unheard for weeks, "keep that vow. Her power inside me is too strong."

"Fight her, brother," said Halberd. "Fight her with all your strength."

"You fight me!" The witch's voice screamed through Labrans' mouth. Labrans reached up to tear Hrungnir from Halberd's grasp. Mälar flattened Labrans with the side of the ax.

"Let me kill him," Mälar said. "He will get one of us yet, I know it."

"Bind him again," Halberd said in disgust. "I cannot yet command this knife sufficiently to break the witch's spell. I know not what to do with my poor brother."

"I know perfectly well," Mälar grumbled. He dragged Labrans across the cave and trussed him like a pig for slaughter. Overhead came the sound of the rock being dragged from the entrance. A loud thump followed.

"Usuthu brings home meat," Mälar said. "Good."

Halberd looked around the cave. All the strips of elk meat were gone.

"By the Gods, Mälar, were you so bored that all you could do was eat?"

"How long do you think you have been gone, young shaman? One week! One full week in this cave with your enchanted brother babbling love talk in that witch's voice. One week of Usuthu chanting and leaving me here alone while he visited his family in a trance. One full week."

Halberd raised a hand to his cheeks. His beard was fuller. His belly was empty.

Three deerskins packed with only the choicest parts crashed onto the floor. Usuthu dropped in behind them.

"The Skrælings," he said, "are everywhere. They know we have not fled their territory. They track us day and night."

"How many did you kill?" Halberd asked.

"No more than twenty. Last night I slept in the trees. Just before dawn I crept into a longhouse and took the head from every other sleeping warrior. These heads I placed beside the sleeping skins of the Skrælings whom I spared. When those awake I think they might lose their stomach for this fight."

"How long were you out of the cave?"

"Only three days and nights. The old man said he preferred to be alone. I could not stand the confinement."

Usuthu smiled. "I am relaxed and content," he said. "I am ready to travel."

"We will not travel, my brothers," Halberd said. "I have another journey to make. I will go to Niflheim. The time has come to rescue my brother from the clutches of Hel."

Mälar and Usuthu exchanged glances.

"Must I recite to you," Mälar said, "all the good reasons against such a trip? Not the least of which is that you will not return. No mortal returns. Those who explore there forfeit the option."

"None of them," Halberd said, "bear Hrungnir."

"All the more reason," said Labrans. "That knife is hers. She wants it back. She will tear you into bits and keep your soul in bondage forever."

Halberd said, "When I have studied the knife and the Jewel of Kyrwyn-Coyne and understand their linked power, then I shall go."

"How will you travel there?" asked Usuthu. "Does Niflheim exist and remain in one place, or is it a spiritual province that may be found only in the Dream World?"

"It is an actual place. Dead souls are consigned there, for eternity. It exists in the bowels of the Earth."

"Do you walk there?"

"Dead spirits are carried there. How the living travel I know not. I believe it can only be done by a spell. I will cast this spell using Hrungnir. But you are correct, Mälar. I dare not bear Hrungnir to that awful place. I must find a way to be protected by the knife even though I do not carry it."

Nothing more needed to be said. Over the protests of Usuthu and Halberd, Mälar climbed out of the cave. Usuthu moved the giant rock so the old man could roam around. Mälar's restlessness tormented him.

Halberd sat by the fire, turning Hrungnir over and over in his hands. He related to Usuthu all that Thessah had told him. Usuthu raised his head. He appeared to be scenting the wind like a hound. He sat with his head upraised for hours, never speaking.

Halberd knew that Usuthu listened to the spirit voices of his people. Usuthu would remember every magical lesson he had ever learned. Perhaps he could recall something that might aid Halberd. Mälar returned, out of breath and bearing a clutch of tender game birds, all skinned and gutted.

"You remained exposed aboveground long enough to kill and skin these birds?" asked Halberd. "Has boredom made you so foolhardy?"

"I chose a shorter route to dinner," Mälar replied. "I came upon a small party of Skrælings who were cleaning their birds after a successful hunt. Alas, they failed to post sentries. More foolishly than that, they engaged me in hand-to-hand combat. Tedium makes my sword faster and sharpens my wits."

"Where lie these bird killers?"

"Just above our cave mouth. Usuthu, I think you should scurry to the hole and pull the rock over. I cannot budge it."

Usuthu stood.

"And, Usuthu," Mälar said, "I would hurry. A rather large force heard the screams of those I fought. They rush this way, eager for our blood."

Usuthu was out the entry hole in two steps. The scraping of the rock being moved echoed through the cave.

"So," said Halberd, "you sought to drive us from this cave? You are devious, helmsman."

"Shaman," Mälar said, "I fear we will never see

you again. I would not have you die in this manner. Is not your quest for the witch more important than your dead brother? He will dwell in Niflheim for eternity, Halberd. Eternity. You could live twenty more years and it would be but the blink of an eye for Valdane's soul. Let him play out his destiny. You must follow yours."

Usuthu returned, smiling broadly.

"Those three who saw me, I slew," he said. "Those fifty or sixty who did not, I left puzzled."

"How many?" Halberd said.

"Many villages have given up their warriors in search of us. We could not leave this rabbit warren if we chose to. So, old man, relax. We have nowhere to go."

"I am relaxed," Mälar said, indicating Labrans bound hand and foot, "now."

Usuthu drew Mälar and Halberd into a tight circle. He spoke in a whisper.

"Halberd, I studied on your problem long and hard. The voices of my ancestors say that the jewel and the knife must work in conjunction. Otherwise, why would they fall into the hands of the same mortal?

"You are fulfilling an ancient prophesy. All evidence points to it; you stole the jewel from the most powerful shaman on earth, you stole the knife from an Immortal. Great wheels are turning and you stand at their center.

"My advice is simple: Unite the knife and the jewel. Unite them and rejoice in the consequences, for those consequences are your fate and your fate alone."

Mälar looked away, shaking his head.

"I am not a spiritual man," he said. "The sea offers too much luck, good and bad, to all comers. In all my years I have discerned no pattern nor guiding hand to the life of men in this world. Gods are Gods and men are men. Yet you, Halberd, a man, have somehow achieved possession of the tools of gods. Usuthu must be correct."

"Unite these two objects," Mälar continued, "and stand aside."

Halberd pulled his broadsword from its shoulder scabbard. The Jewel of Kyrwyn-Coyne, resting in its intricately woven nest of fine silver, glowed like a tiny bonfire.

"Behold!" Halberd cried. "Your words have set the jewel alight. The Forces speak through this jewel to all of us. Your counsel is wise. I shall follow it without delay."

Though it pained his heart, Halberd pulled his dagger and twisted its point into the nest that held the jewel. The smiths who lived on the Guardian Rock in the Inland Sea had made that fine silver-work. It had survived many battles. Halberd picked at it carefully, making only the smallest tear.

He pried one strand apart. Working with his fingers, he loosened the threads of silver one at a time. It was not easy for him to deface this handiwork. The delicate and perfect balance of his broadsword would also be affected by the removal of the jewel. No matter. Sweat ran down his forehead. Usuthu passed him chunks of deer heart as he worked. Halberd gulped down his first nourishment in a week without tasting it.

The jewel rolled free. Halberd slid the sword back into its scabbard and his dagger into the sheath sewn on the lower back of his leather chest armor. He held the jewel in his palm for the first time in years.

The power of the jewel coursed through him. The jewel glowed, as if waiting for a command.

"Am I wrong," Halberd wondered aloud, "all these years? I always regarded the jewel as a telltale, a confirmation device. What if it carries strengths I've never attempted to tap?"

"You'll know soon," Mälar said. He eyed the jewel nervously.

Halberd lifted Hrungnir to eye level. He studied the scooped-out hole in the top. Into this hole Grettir had splashed Valdane's blood. With that blood she had toasted Halberd. His brother's blood had run down her chin as she drank from the knife.

Halberd held the jewel near the hole. As he pushed the jewel toward the hole, the knife jumped from his hand as if alive. It bounced along the cave floor with loud scraping sound. Halberd picked the knife off the floor. Usuthu and Mälar looked on, barely breathing.

Again Halberd held the jewel to the scooped-out hole in the top of Hrungnir. He gripped the knife tightly. As the jewel neared the knife, each seemed to repel the other. They did not want to touch.

Some invisible force separated them, pushed them apart. Halberd shoved, but the two would not touch.

Halberd held them as close together as he could. About six inches of air separated them.

"Hrungnir, do my bidding," Halberd shouted. "Combine with this jewel and place me in the center of your joined power! I am Halberd, Shaman of the Northmen, I own you, Hrungnir and the jewel as well. You are my spoils—do my bidding, now!"

"Now!" Mälar shouted.

"Now!" called Usuthu.

"Bear me to Niflheim and protect me on my journey," Halberd commanded.

Usuthu drew the magic hammer from around his neck. He smote the ground in front of Halberd with all his strength. The cave floor cracked in a long, crazy line. The fissure raced across the floor. From far below came the sound of creaking and tearing, the sound of branches breaking and leaves rustling. The noise grew louder and louder.

"Halberd, beware!" Mälar cried.

The jewel ceased resisting Halberd's pressure, as did Hrungnir. As the jewel neared its resting place at the top of the knife, the sound of whipping branches and blowing leaves drew nearer. When the jewel touched the knife both leaped from Halberd's hands. A great wind knocked Halberd flat on his back.

The floor of the cave burst upward.

The jewel and Hrungnir, locked together but never touching, floated in the air directly above Halberd.

The uppermost branches of a great tree crashed

through the fissure in the floor. The force of the tree tossed chunks of stone and cave floor throughout the cave. Usuthu and Mãlar rolled onto their sides, wrapping their heads in their arms. The branches reached to the top of the cave. The leaves whipped and tossed as if a hurricane blew through the cave.

A soft golden light radiated from the jewel and the knife. The glow formed a golden circle. The glowing ring floated lazily in the cave, hovering over Halberd.

Halberd raised his arms to the glowing golden light, embracing it like a lover. The light surrounded him, molding to his shape. Halberd stood. He glowed with the same light. It danced around him. His arms and legs dazzled. When he moved, the light moved with him. Halberd was aglow, ablaze, alight; he was enchanted and protected.

Halberd reached one golden, blazing arm towards Hrungnir and the jewel. They floated higher, just out of his reach. Halberd drew his broadsword. It, too, was lined with golden light, and sparkled in the cave.

Halberd examined his arms and legs with wonder, laughing like a child.

"All this knowledge," he cried. "All this power under my very nose, and I ignored it. Brothers, greater prizes than revenge over the witch await us in this Unknown World."

He laughed again.

"Remember your mother's warning," Usuthu shouted over the crackling of the leaves. "You will be tempted with power. Do not become drunk on it. Bend it to your needs, bend not yourself to it."

"Aye," Halberd laughed drunkenly, "aye, my brother, you are so right. But leave me this moment to be drunk on it. Leave me this one moment of infinite earthly power."

Usuthu raised his tiny silver mallet over his head.

"Renounce the joy you feel, my brother! Remember your quest and renounce this lust for power. Swear you will bend this power to your will."

"Or what, Mongol?" Halberd spoke with his eyes contemptuously slitted.

"Or else I shall break your magical shield with this mallet and slay you where you stand. Worlds crack open for you, yet you behave like a child."

Usuthu braced his feet. His jaw was set.

Mälar raised the ax. He looked from Northman to Mongol and back again. Labrans lay in the corner, his eyes wide open, Grettir observing the scene through her captive's eyes.

Halberd lowered his head. Long moments passed. When he raised his head again his voice and eyes were those of a true shaman.

"Intoxication is delightful, my brother," he said quietly. "But it is not a warrior's way. I am ready to be responsible to this great power. I will not be tempted again."

"If you are," Usuthu said, "then you will be. Temptation is not evil. Succumbing to it is. You tread where mortal man has never walked. The temptations in your path will be monstrous. Use your strength and resist."

"What," asked Mälar, "of this fiendish tree?"

"Know you nothing, old man? This is Yggdrasil, the Tree of Life. Its roots run straight down to Niflheim. My spell has brought it to me. I shall climb down its branches and confront Hel." Halberd gazed about the cave. "Fare you well, Usuthu. And you, Mälar. Do not kill Labrans if you can avoid it. I will see you soon."

"Fare you well, Halberd." They had spoken together.

Halberd returned his broadsword to its scabbard. He swung into the branches of Yggdrasil. The wind increased, whipping the branches sideways. Halberd held on. The wind subsided.

Halberd waved good-bye and began to climb down. He climbed below the level of the cave floor. The tree shifted again. Halberd wrapped his glowing arms around the slender trunk and gripped tightly.

With a monstrous creaking and groaning, the tree raced downward. Above Halberd's head the ruptured stone floor of the cave slammed shut like a trap.

Yggdrasil stopped moving. Halberd found himself in a dark passageway lit only by tiny streams of light. He climbed carefully downward. He could see nothing around the tree. For hours and hours he climbed. Halberd lost track of time. He climbed down until no light at all showed. The glow surrounding his body grew brighter. Still, he climbed.

He passed into Midgard. Surrounding the tree were thousands of Giants and Dwarfs, each more horrible to behold than the last. Curiously, they did not notice the puny mortal climbing in their midst. They ate, drank, fought and caroused, ignoring Halberd all the while.

This glowing enchantment grants me the cloak of invisibility, Halberd thought. None may see the Tree of Life but those who have called for it.

Day turned to night and night into day and still Halberd climbed downward through Midgard. The sun did not rise and set in this land of Giants and Dwarfs. Instead, three golden-haired maidens sailed across the stone sky of this middle-earth land, riding in a chariot pulled by three black wolves. As Halberd knew, no Dwarf could bear the rays of the sun. Thund had been able to fight Halberd in broad daylight only because he had assumed the form of a Skræling.

Halberd climbed until Midgard disappeared. Yggdrasil reached below him to bottomless depths. He climbed through black rocky caverns and rich valleys cut with frothing rivers. He climbed through low-ceilinged caves forested with bats and he climbed through vast damp jungles. Yggdrasil floated amidst these strange worlds, in them but not of them. After the bats, Halberd saw not another living thing.

As he climbed it grew colder and colder. First his breath appeared. Then his fingertips grew numb. Then his breath froze in midair as it left his mouth and crashed to the ground, where it broke and scattered like fine crystal hurled into a fireplace.

Still Halberd climbed down.

Huge stalactites of gray, dirty ice hung from every rock. Yggdrasil grew slippery with ice. Every branch was coated with rime.

Halberd climbed the icy branches until the roots of Yggdrasil appeared below him. He was near the entrance to Niflheim. Here would he take great, great care.

Halberd drew his sword as he stepped from the roots of Yggdrasil. With his glowing sword Halberd traced an X into the air. It hung before him, glowing golden and true.

"Hang here," Halberd commanded, "and mark my way back to Yggdrasil, wherever the Tree of Life may be."

As Halberd walked he occasionally marked the gray rock on which he trod with a slash of his golden sword. The golden marks beckoned him back to the Tree. He ignored their call.

The rock ended abruptly. Below his feet was a cliff too high to measure. At its base tumbled Authun, the river over which the dead must sail to gain entrance to Niflheim. The river tossed and twisted, throwing white water high over huge rocks.

Long icicles hung from the cliff. The edges of Authun were frozen into thick plates of gray ice. The river wound its narrow, fearsome course through this ice. Here and there, huge black rocks coated with ice thrust up through the sheets covering the riverbanks.

As Halberd watched, a ghostly vessel floated down Authun, tossing and turning on its heaving surface. An ancient, wizened Northman guided the ships' tiller.

"Old man," Halberd shouted down from the clifftop. "Old man, may I ride on your ship to the gates of Niflheim? I must speak with Hel."

None of the ship's passengers gave any sign of hearing Halberd. They wrapped their arms around their chests and slapped their hands, all in a vain search for warmth. Long strands of filthy ice hung from every rope and spar. The decks were coated and slippery.

The old man raised his head. His dead eyes showed no surprise at the sight of Halberd standing on the cliff, glowing with golden light.

"Young man," he called, "you are not dead, are you?"

"No, old man, I live."

"Young man," the old man called, "you are not immortal, are you?"

"No," Halberd said, "one day I shall die."

"In that case, young man, you may not ride with me or with any ship that plies the waters of Authun. Good-bye."

The old man turned his attention to the raging waters. The ship sailed down the ferocious canyon. Halberd surveyed the wide cliffs that stood on either side of Authun. He looked far down the waters but could not see the entrance to the cave that guarded Niflheim.

Halberd raised his broadsword in a two-handed grip. He smote the edge of the cliff with the glowing blade. The shock of the impact threw Halberd backward. A rumbling filled the air.

The wall split like a ripe fruit. Huge stones

sprayed out, falling into the river and sailing beyond its banks. Ice-covered rocks tumbled to the river's edge, forming a broken staircase. The cliff edge held the golden glow of Halberd's sword.

Halberd struggled down the slick rocks. When he reached the thick ice on Authun's banks, he fell roughly and slid straight for the roiling water. Halberd drove his dagger into the ice and held fast.

He lay on the ice, contemplating his course. There was only one way to travel on such a surface. Halberd stood with care. Making long, sliding steps, he began to move quickly down the riverside. Soon he was swooping down the bank, pushing with one foot and then the other, never lifting his feet from the ice, never stopping.

Halberd slid along the ice for leagues upon leagues. Every breath he let out froze in the air and floated behind him like a white cloud. Though ice hung from every rock and a freezing wind tore at his face, the cold never pierced his golden armor. His arms and legs never tired. Ahead, he could see the entrance to the cave. Reaching from the cave to the river was a rotting pier of ramshackle gray wood coated with the same filthy ice. Halberd slid to the pillars that supported the dock and gained its surface.

A roaring growl filled the cavern, drowning out the roar of the river. A fiendish black hound, his eyes blind and his teeth dripping vile foam, sprang from the cave entrance and launched himself at Halberd.

Halberd had only time to raise his dagger and fall

back. The hound leaped for Halberd's throat. His first great rush carried him flying over Halberd as he landed flat on his back on the rickety dock. The hound whirled and bounded at Halberd again.

Halberd recognized him in that instant. It was Garm, the immortal dog that guarded the cave. As Garm charged, Halberd knelt on the dock. He held his glowing dagger toward the hound of Niflheim. Garm paused, sniffing the air and digging in his heels on the rotting wooden planking.

Halberd drew a small circle in the air with the point of his dagger.

"Bind this hound!" he cried.

Garm sprang. His head passed through the floating golden circle. It snapped shut around Garm's neck. He fell to the deck, whimpering and pulling at his new golden collar with his front paws. Halberd stood. He shifted his dagger to his left hand and drew his broadsword with his right. He trod the dock gingerly, looking all around him.

Now would come his severest test. Hel would not answer his challenge so rapidly. She would send her servants to dispatch Halberd. If she feared him she would send Niddhog, the Great Serpent.

It would be unwise policy to answer the appearance of one mortal with Hel's strongest ally. That would show fear, something Gods were not wont to do. If she considered Halberd only a nuisance, Hel would send whatever warrior guarded her gate.

Halberd peered into the blackness of the cave that led to the entrance to Niflheim. A ghostly Northman clad in armor and bearing a sword and a mace shuffled from the blackness of the cave into the halflight. Halberd's heart sank when he saw the guardian. Halberd was trapped by Hel's diabolical cunning.

The guardian warrior was his dead brother, Valdane.

Valdane raised his sword. Halberd knew he could not speak. Valdane's tongue had been torn out before his death. He had lost the gift of speech for all eternity.

"Valdane, it is your brother, Halberd, come to free you from Hel. Do not kill me. Hear my plan instead."

Valdane's ghost shook its gray, translucent head. Its expression did not change. Halberd had never bested his brother in combat. No mortal had. Valdane would surely kill him now, enchantment or no.

Halberd backed up several steps. Valdane did not advance onto the dock. Apparently his duty was to protect the entrance of the cave.

"Ragnarok!" Halberd screamed into the raging river. "Ragnarok, come to me now and pay your debt. Come to this place and fulfill your vow."

A Giant appeared on the end of the dock. He was as big as five Northmen. His head was covered with gashes and scars. His arms were knotty with muscle. His red beard carried its own light. The brown eye in the center of his forehead showed little pity but, somehow, much humor. He bore a Giant's dagger and a war club made from a thick branch. He wore only a skirt of red cloth and a thick band of gold around his wrist.

"How dare you, mortal, summon me to this awful place. What vow do I owe you?"

"I am Halberd. It was I who freed you and your fellows from the hump of the Dwarf, Thund. You swore to aid me, once only. Now I call upon you for that aid."

"Ahhh ... so it is you, mortal. Aye, your name is famous in Midgard. You slew an Immortal. Some would smash you for it, Some would grant you immortality. Indeed. I am in your debt. I will give you aid. What do you wish?"

"Gain me access to Hel. Gain me also safe passage from this place."

"That, mortal, is two things. I will aid you only in one."

"Aid me in my safe return, then."

"I shall. That is a wise choice. You do not need me to see the Goddess. Can you not fight your way in?"

"Hel is too clever for me. She knew I was coming. She placed my dead brother here at the entrance as her guard. She knows I cannot harm him. My heart would not allow it. Neither would his sword arm."

"Why does he not speak?"

"He has no tongue. The Dwarf Suttung tore it out."

"Ah." The Giant's voice boomed like thunder around the cavern.

"Tell me, Ragnarok, are you a ghost of the Giant I released from the Dwarf's hump, or do you live?"

"I live. I was not slain by Thund, but badly hurt.

Thund stabbed us and cut us badly. While we suffered he enslaved us by a spell and hid us in his hump. We rotted there for centuries before you set us free. It is not easy to kill an Immortal. It can be done, but it is not easy."

"Does this mean," Halberd said in horror, "that Thund is not slain? Does he walk the Earth, seeking revenge on me?"

"No, mortal. You slew him with one of the few tools that may do the job. Hrungnir can send an Immortal from this world and leave no trace."

Halberd turned back to his brother. The ghost ventured not one step onto the dock. Another sailing ship negotiated Authun's tortured waters. The wretched cargo of gray souls, all marching with their heads down, filed past the Giant and Halberd on the dock. They gave no sign of noticing. Valdane stood aside and let them pass.

"Mortal," spake Ragnarok, "you have entertained me today. I bear no particular love for Hel. She stood by while Thund made me a prisoner. She is born of those in Aasgard as well as those of Midgard, yet she bows to Odin and offers no aid to her half-brothers.

"Perhaps I can help you. I would enjoy tricking the Goddess. I will aid you for my own amusement. When it ceases to amuse me, I will cease. At that time you may have your safe passage home. If you refuse it at that exact moment you must forfeit my vow."

Halberd calculated quickly. If the Giant were in

league with Hel, this could be his undoing. But how could he be? Hel used Dwarfs as her servants, never Giants. Hel's mother had been a Giant, yet Hel hated the Giants and had never questioned Odin's edict that cast her into Niflheim. To the proud Giants, who were constantly at war with the Gods, this was craven cowardice. Or, even worse, it showed a desire to join the Gods and reject the Giants.

Halberd nodded his head. The Giant stepped to the entrance of the cave.

"Ghost," Ragnarok said to Halberd's brother, "do you guard this gate?"

The ghost of Valdane nodded.

"Do you bar the way to all?"

The ghost shook its empty head.

"Do you bar the way to mortals who still live?"

The ghost nodded.

"To Immortals?"

Valdane shook his head.

"Are you under a spell?"

It nodded.

"Do you recognize this presumptuous mortal at my side?"

Again it nodded.

"Has Hel charged you with slaying him?"

The ghost nodded sadly.

"Must you obey?"

And again.

Ragnarok turned to Halberd.

"You will not pass this point, mortal. Odin grants

Hel the right to guard her gate. To enter by force is to defy his will."

Halberd lowered his head and his sword. His journey had come to naught.

"Hel!" called the Giant. "Come and speak to the Giant, Ragnarok. Come forth and make a trade with me. I bear a great prize."

Halberd looked to the cave mouth expectantly. An oozing, slithering sound rose, echoing through the cavern. It drowned out Authun. It drowned out the whines of Garm.

Ragnarok grinned at Halberd, his one eye glowing.

"Now, mortal," he said, "we shall see how strong you are. Behold the foulest thing that moves in all the Worlds."

The slithering grew louder. The sound of scales upon rock rose from the cave.

Halberd, now truly worried, turned to the Giant. He could see no higher than the Giant's knee.

"Is this Niddhog? Does she unleash the Serpent upon us?"

"You are brave, mortal, but appallingly ignorant. Watch the cave mouth and see what living mortals never see."

A head emerged from the cave. It was not serpent, but not human. It had eyes, a nose and a mouth, but no ears. One half of the face was dead. On that side, black, rotting skin hung in strips. An eye dangled out of the face on a bouncing stalk. Pus oozed from the dead eye socket, coating the stalk and dripping down the long, long scaly neck.

The half that wasn't dead was covered with scales. Human arms and hands grew from a thick snake's body, which bulged on the ground and ended in fins like a dragon's and large flippers, like a seal's, instead of feet. All the way down this horrid form, dead skin hung. Fishbelly-white, dead flesh showed below the black, hanging strips. The fingers on the living, scale-coated hand ended in giant curving claws. The beast stank of death, rot, moldering corpses and something even worse than all of those.

"Ragnarok," she spoke, "you speak of a prize. What is it and what do you want for it?"

Her voice sounded like a burning corpse rolling down wet cobblestones. It bumped and slithered. In her voice gathered all the anguish of every soul in Niflheim, coupled with Hel's own boredom with an eternity of their screams. Her voice wrapped around Halberd's ears, filling him with deep despair. It inspired nothingness. It called for suicide.

"Do not speak to her," the Giant said to Halberd behind an upraised hand. "She will enslave you."

"Hel," Ragnarok said, "behold this thick gold bracelet upon my wrist. Every day it sheds eleven bracelets identical to itself. Every day eleven times this great band of gold I add to my riches. I will trade it to you."

Hel turned her one living eye onto Halberd. Her gaze burned through him. He raised his golden broadsword to deflect the beam. When she saw the golden weapon she hissed in frustration. Rock fell from the cliffs behind them at the sound. Halberd's blood froze in his veins.

When his blood moved once more, his heart thumped like a drum. Halberd shook with fear.

Her slithering voice, making the sound no one may hear when a serpent's tongue tests the air, spoke with bitter resignation.

"Now I know you do not bring me the one thing on this earth I desire. What do I want with gold?"

"I care not what you would do with it, Hel," spake Ragnarok. "Perhaps you might use it to pay the Dwarfs at their smithy to forge you whatever object you like.

"I will swap my endless supply of gold for this pathetic ghost here, who stands guard at your cave and will not advance onto this miserable dock."

Hel's breath left her mouth with a drawn-out hiss. It poured over the ground, wet and smoky, freezing and still hot enough to burn.

Halberd held his golden sword before him and the evil mist parted to go around him. It boiled up, blinding him to Ragnarok and Hel. It smelled of corpses older than time, and of evil repaid a thousand times over. None of it touched him.

"You dare to mock me, Giant? You dare to aid this mortal against me? I will never set this ghost free, except in return for one item and that item was taken from me. I want Hrungnir. By rights, it is mine. If not Hrungnir, then I want this red-bearded mortal who cowers beside you."

Halberd felt her words go through him like a knife.

Ignoring the Giant's advice, Halberd stepped forward, his golden sword before him.

Ragnarok reached down and took Halberd by the back of his armor with a thumb and forefinger. He held the Northman in his place.

"Thank you for your time, Hel," Ragnarok said. "We shall be on our way." He pulled Halberd's tunic with his huge hand, lifting the Viking slightly off his feet.

Halberd shook himself from the Giant's grasp. Shifting his golden three-sided stabbing dagger into his right hand, he strode toward the horrible goddess.

"Come forward, ugly hag, and take me yourself! Do not insist that others do your work for you," Halberd shouted. "I cower to no one and no thing, mortal or immortal, God or man, living or dead! I bow down to Thor, and Thor only. True, I fear death. I also fear Grettir and I fear the evil that lurks in my heart, as it lurks in every mortal's.

"But, foul bitch, I do not fear you!"

Halberd drew the dagger behind his head, and, throwing himself forward, he hurled the enchanted dirk at Hel with all his might. Valdane's ghost bore no shield; he could only watch the knife slice through the freezing air.

Hel squawked like a giant bird and cocked her head to the side, but she had not been attacked by anything or anyone for thousands of years. She had lost the knack of fighting. The dagger flew true and hard, guided by enchantment and Halberd's strength.

The golden blade struck Hel just below her dangling eye. Thick green pus spurted from the wound. The pus shot out in a stream, coursing down Hel's scaly flank. Hel raised her awful head high and screamed in a searing, screeching voice. She flopped towards Halberd and Ragnarok.

"Time," said the Giant, "to go."

He took Halberd up into his huge palm and nestled him there.

"Ragnarok, my dagger and my brother's ghost!"

Halberd looked back at Hel. Somehow she had grown to twice her size of an instant ago. She raced out of the cave. As she gallumphed onto the dock like a terrible seal, Hel kicked Valdane back into the cave with one twitch of her enormous flipper. The ghost disappeared into the blackness of Niflheim.

"Valdane!"

It was too late. The ghost of his brother was gone, beyond rescue.

"Ragnarok, I am not safe without that dagger. Hel might use the enchantment it bears against me. Fulfill your vow and retrieve it."

Ragnarok raised his huge war club. When Hel reached near them the Giant struck. He lashed her on her side opposite the knife wound. Hel rolled squawking to the dock. Ragnarok snaked out one quick hand and plucked the dagger from Hel's head. She screamed louder than ever. Halberd felt blood run from his ears. It poured down his neck and froze in the cold.

Ragnarok handed the dagger to Halberd. The Giant could barely grip it, it was so tiny. He held it gingerly between his fingernails. Halberd sheathed the dirk.

Hel rolled to her upright position with great difficulty. Pus still ran from the wound in her neck. Her dangling eye bounced as she struggled to raise her long neck and foul head. As the pus struck the frozen ground each drop became a lost soul, gray and weeping, empty and tormented forever.

Ragnarok wasted no time. He whirled and leaped from the end of the dock onto the ice on the other side of Authun. His huge foot grazed another gray ship that had just reached the dock. The ship spilled its doomed souls into the freezing waters. In an eyeblink they and the ship were swept from sight.

Hel screamed again at this loss.

Ragnarok hit the ice running. His huge strides ate the distance. Leagues that had taken Halberd hours to slide Ragnarok raced over in minutes. They could no longer see Hel. Ahead the golden rocks glowed.

"Run up that rock staircase and look for golden signs," Halberd shouted. "There we will find Yggdrasil."

Ragnarok had one foot on the broken glowing rocks that led to the top of the cliff. As he planted his foot to climb, the rocks exploded back into his face. Ragnarok was hurled to the opposite bank of Authun. He landed on his back with a crash. Halberd flew from one side of the Giant's fist to the other. He knelt on the callused palm, fighting for breath and trying to regain his senses.

Ragnarok swung onto his knees, resting his hands on the ground beside. Again Halberd tumbled across the Giant's hand. Through the Giant's closed fingers he saw Ragnarok raise his head. The Giant smiled bitterly.

He stood. Halberd tumbled again. The Giant spake one word.

"Niddhog."

Halberd stood and peered through the bars of the Giant's fingers. Emerging from the broken staircase of rock across the river, its head poking up through solid rock, was the great serpent itself.

"Do not join this fight, mortal," Ragnarok said calmly. "The serpent belongs to me."

"No, Ragnarok, I must."

Ragnarok simply opened his hand. Halberd fell from the palm and thumped into the icy ground. All the breath left his body. He gasped on the shore of the eternal river, watching as the Giant raised his club and stepped right into the frozen torrent.

Niddhog struck from the rocks, shooting its long, winged neck out of the cliff. Its huge jaws gaped. Rows of dripping teeth opened. Its front claws reached for the Giant.

Ragnarok braced his feet against the slippery, ice-coated bottom of Authun and swung his huge club. The rounded head struck the dragon just above its wings. Niddhog was thrown back against the cliff. Its rear claws came free of the rocks. It clutched the top of the cliff with them and sent off a plume of flame from its mouth straight into the face of Ragnarok.

The Giant scooped a huge palmful of frigid water from Authun and hurled it into the path of the flame. The doused flames vanished. The wave of water, which became ice as it traveled through the air, broke across the dragon's face, confusing it.

Ragnarok stepped in behind his wall of ice and bashed the dragon over its head. Niddhog lost its grip on the cliff and fell forward. As it did, it lashed out with its front claws, sinking them deeply into the Giant's bare chest. Niddhog flapped its scaly wings. It was trying to lift Ragnarok off the ground.

Ragnarok raised his head to the heavens and roared with pain. The air was filled with the hideous beating of leathery wings. Ragnarok dropped his club and seized the dragon around its neck. Though the Giant was as tall as five men, his great hands barely encircled the dragon's thick throat.

Ragnarok choked the beast. He beat its head against the cliff. Rocks broke from the cliff at the impact.

Niddhog responded by raising its back claws and slashing forward. It was trying to gut the Giant, trying to plant those huge claws into Ragnarok's belly.

Ragnarok ignored the blood pouring from his chest. He stepped sideways to avoid the back claws and slammed Niddhog's head into the cliff again. A rock as big as a Northman village broke from the cliff and landed in the middle of Authun, soaking Halberd with a great splash of ice.

Halberd raised his arm against the falling ice. He ran for the river. He leaped from his bank onto the side of the huge rock. He ran across its crest and scampered down the other side. From there a gentle hop carried Halberd to the side of Authun on which the battle raged.

Niddhog ignored Halberd. He swung his enchanted sword at the lower legs of the dragon. Halberd cleanly chopped off three clawed toes from one of Niddhog's slashing feet. Blood spurted out, soaking Halberd. The purple blood instantly froze. Halberd slashed at himself with his dagger, breaking his cloak of purple ice. He beat his limbs against his chest. The ice cracked and fell away.

Niddhog twisted its head downward, trying to see its new enemy. It pulled its front claws from Ragnarok's chest. Strips of bloody flesh came free with the claws. Blood gouted onto the cliffs. Ragnarok seized the moment and hurled the dragon across the river.

Niddhog hit hard. Instead of bounding back and attacking, the dragon curled its head down and licked its ruined foot. Its royal purple blood dripped onto the ice and instantly froze. Every time Niddhog laid its foot on the ice the freezing blood held it fast. The dragon rolled onto its side and held its foot above the ice. Niddhog glared with hate and frustration across the river. It shot a breath of flame at the Giant and the shaman. The flame barely reached their side of the river.

The Giant examined his chest. He was badly mauled. Claw marks scored his chest to the bone. His ribs glinted beneath his torn flesh. His blood froze as it pumped out, forming a reddish-white cloak of bloody ice around his chest.

"Ragnarok," asked Halberd, "can you be slain by these wounds?"

"Yes, mortal," the Giant gasped. "Niddhog serves a Goddess. He may slay Immortals, though he is seldom called upon to do so. My blood pours out of me. I am gravely wounded. But, do not fear, my vow shall be fulfilled. Let us climb."

He picked Halberd from the ice and stumbled up the rocky staircase. From there he followed the golden marks to the base of Yggdrasil. The Tree of Life stretched above them. There was no end to its branches.

"Climb into my hair, Halberd," the Giant commanded. "I require both arms to climb."

Halberd climbed to the Giant's shoulder and wrapped his hands into Ragnarok's hair. The Giant climbed easily and tirelessly. His wounds did not seem to affect him. They soared upward, past the valleys and rivers, through the jungles and even through Midgard. The Giant never stopped.

When they had climbed to the bottom of the blackest vaults, so that no light shown on the branches above, Ragnarok halted. He sat on a large branch and lowered his head.

"I must rest," he said. "I have not much more blood in my body."

Halberd looked below them for the first time. Down as far as he could see, Yggdrasil was smeared with the Giant's blood. The unbroken stripe of fluid reached into the darkness.

"Brave Giant," Halberd said, "let me try to stem your bleeding with my enchanted sword. It has powers I do not yet know. Perhaps it may close the wounds from a dragon.''

"I am Ragnarok" the Giant roared. "I take no aid from mortals. If I must die fulfilling my vow then so be it. If I survive this day it is because you saved my life. Do not ask me to debase myself. Say no more.''

Ragnarok motioned again to Halberd. The Viking climbed onto the Giant's shoulders. The Giant flew up the Tree of Life and gained the top. The cold stone roof above them showed no opening. Ragnarok drew back one huge fist and beat on the rock. It did not open.

Halberd scrambled from the Giant's shoulders to the top of his head. Halberd raised his sword.

"Open in the name of Thor! Open for two brave warriors who have been to Niflheim and live to tell the tale. Open for me, Halberd, Dream Warrior!"

Halberd smashed his sword into the rock above his head. The blade vanished into the rock wall as if the wall were made of butter. He felt the blade break through to the other side. He wrenched his sword free and swung again. A tiny crack appeared.

Halberd slid down the Giant's neck to his ear.

"Brace yourself, brave Ragnarok," Halberd whispered, "and drive your head through this opening I have chopped.''

Halberd jumped off the Giant and wrapped his hands in the branches of Yggdrasil. Ragnarok gripped the branches to either side of himself. He set his feet in the junction of other branches. He lowered into a squat, blood pumping from his ruined chest as he did.

He surged up out of the squat, fast as a tiger springing onto its prey. His huge head crashed into the rock ceiling, smack into the glowing golden line carved by Halberd's sword.

His head burst through, hurling rocks into the air that crashed back down around the top of his head. His one great eye slid above the level of the cave floor.

Regarding him with fear and loathing were Usuthu and Mälar. Mälar held a Eerhahkwoi lance high, ready to strike. Usuthu held his bow tightly drawn, ready to fire. Both were frozen with wonder.

"Do not harm this Giant," Halberd's voice carried from below them. "He is our friend and dies at this moment from wounds suffered on my behalf."

Halberd climbed up Yggdrasil and emerged beside the Giant's head. Ragnarok raised his head into the cave, filling it from the rent in the floor to the top. Mälar's mouth hung open. Usuthu lowered his lance and raised a hand in greeting.

"The vow is now reversed, Ragnarok," said Halberd. "If you survive, and this poor mortal may aid you in any way, I and my friends will be at your side."

"A fine vow, mortal," Ragnarok gasped, "But one with little chance of being performed. I am bathed in my own blood. My ribs gleam in the light from your cook-fire. Niddhog has ripped me to pieces. I will try to climb back to my home in Midgard to die. Fare you well."

"And you, Ragnarok," Halberd answered, but it was too late.

The Giant's head vanished from sight. As Ragnarok climbed down, the top of Yggdrasil slid beneath the floor of the cave. The wind that Yggdrasil carried with it ceased. A few scattered leaves littered the floor.

The sides of the immense tear in the rock floor moved slowly toward one another. The hole closed with the grinding of rock upon rock. The passage to Niflheim was sealed.

On the Shoulders of Giants

Lying on the stone floor of the cave, his golden glow fading, Halberd told of his adventures. As he spoke, he beckoned Hrungnir and the Jewel of Kyrwyn-Coyne down into his hands. They floated near him, casting their golden light. Halberd interrupted himself to call out.

"Knife and jewel, Halberd is returned and the spell is lifted. Separate and fall into my hands."

The two objects leapt apart. The glow vanished. Each hit the stone floor with a clatter.

"Every time you venture forth a new curse descends upon us," laughed Mälar. "It is not enough for you to offend mortals; now you have wounded a Goddess. Her father is merely Loki, the Trickster, and her mother a Giantess. Hel may not venture into this world, but Loki certainly can. Revenge is his specialty.

"Worse, you maimed Niddhog. Pray he cannot travel on dry land. When next we sail the sea he will be waiting for us."

"But, now the Giants know of your quest and

will help us," Usuthu said. "All will know that you saved Ragnarok."

"If I saved him—but I do not think I did. His ribs shined through his torn flesh like teeth. The Gods and Giants have always been at war," Halberd said as he stowed Hrungnir into its holster. "Mortals stand to the side and let them fight. What choice do we have? It will do us no good to be perceived by one side as aiding the other. We are only fodder to them."

Halberd juggled the jewel from hand to hand. He did not know where to carry it. For lack of a better place, he stuffed it inside his leather chest armor.

"We must move west," Mälar said. "The cave falls around our ears."

The cave was littered with boulders. Cracks shot through the walls. The rock ceiling sagged.

"Stone cannot bear all this upheaval," Mälar said. "The floor closed, yes, but the walls and roof bore the strain. Rocks fall onto our heads."

"How many days was I gone?"

"Less than a day and a night," Usuthu replied. "Time in the Underworld must move faster than it does here."

"Aye," Halberd said. "I thought I climbed Yggdrasil for two days and nights, at least. Well, no matter. Have you scouted above?"

"The large Skræling parties seem to have returned to their villages," Usuthu said. "Perhaps they believe we've vanished into the air."

"And so we shall," Halberd said. "Gather the deer and my bound brother. We must ride."

"Ride?" Mälar croaked. "Upon what?"

"Not what, old man, but whom."

The remaining deer was packed into one of the skins. Water skins were filled at the bubbling spring. Usuthu led the way up. He dragged the stone aside and listened to the air carefully. When he believed the way was clear, he climbed from the hole. The Northmen followed.

"We cannot find the falls without guidance from Ishlanawanda," Halberd said, "but too much time have we remained in one spot. I would dream, but I cannot take the time."

Usuthu and Mälar watched the path with care. Halberd raised his hands into the air.

"Urd and Ull," he called, "Giants of Midgard! Come to me now and repay the vow you swore."

Two heads peered down at the explorers from above the nearest tree. These giants were larger even than Ragnarok. The tree fell over with a tearing of roots. The crash echoed through the forest.

"I am Urd," said one.

"And I am Ull. Are you the mortal, Halberd?"

"Yes, it is I who freed you from the Dwarf."

"Make no speeches," grumbled Urd, his voice rumbling like an avalanche in a deep iron mine. "Ragnarok has spoken of your bravery. Also, he says a Giant may be highly amused while in your company."

"And," asked Halberd, "does brave Ragnarok survive?"

"If we remained in Midgard we might know," said Ull. His voice screeched like an owl. It bent and cracked, rising higher and higher. It hurt the ears. "But we were summoned hence. So we know not."

Urd had long, shining black hair, a large drooping belly of fat and flabby arms and shoulders. His pasty white skin could barely be seen through his bearlike pelt of black hair. Those teeth that remained in his head were black and broken. He wore fur leggings like a Northman and a shirt of coarse red cloth. He bore a fighting ax of unimaginable size in one thick-knuckled hand. His ears protruded from his head like handles. Except for his hair, he resembled a Troll. A very, very large Troll. Urd was at least six Northmen tall.

Ull stood as high as Urd's flapping ears. Where Urd's shoulder's sagged, Ull's posture was as erect as a general of the Short-Sword men who lived on the Inland Sea and built stone roads over which they traveled to conquer. His bright yellow hair fell in tangled curls well down his back. His blue eyes rested in a sea of crow's-feet and deep wrinkles. Ull's muscles had the sleek look of a racing hound and he was quite slender. He wore a stabbing dagger in his belt and a broadsword upright over his shoulder, the handle rising above his head, much like the shoulder scabbard in which Halberd bore his sword. He wore a long multicolored robe. It resembled the garb of the slave traders on the Inland Sea. The buckle that bound his belt was a large skull. It appeared to be the skull of a Dwarf.

Ull's features were regular and pleasing, unusual for a Giant. He kept his eyes on the horizon and his nose in the air, searching for trouble and reading the wind.

Mälar, never at a loss for words, called up to the blonde Giant.

"Ull, great Giant, are you a sailor on the seas of Midgard? You have the countenance and bearing of a sailor."

"Yes," Ull answered in his breaking, birdlike voice. "I sail the seas of all worlds, not just Midgard. I have sailed all the waters of this world many times."

"Is your ship visible to mortals?" the navigator asked.

"At times."

"Why," interrupted Urd in his deep voice, "have we been called here?"

"Giants," said Halberd, "I will not recount your vow to me, you know it well. We must gain the Thundering Falls at the Place Where the Lakes You May Not See Across Meet. We know not where it is. We have little time.

"I charge you, therefore, to fulfill your vow. Bear us to this falls as rapidly as you may."

"You come cheap, mortal," mumbled Urd. "Ragnarok gained the adventure of several lifetimes and us you would use as pack dogs."

"Do not speak too soon," answered Halberd. "Adventure may yet come your way. Will you help us?"

"Do not speak back to us!" thundered Urd. "We have sworn a vow. We shall fulfill it. You cannot solve your own problems, mortal, so we have come to solve them for you."

Urd and Ull were astonished to see the mortals draw their weapons as one and assume a fighting stance. Usuthu trained his arrow on one of Ull's bright blue eyes. Halberd raised his broadsword and Mälar, the ax. None showed any fear.

"We have sailed the world, great Giants," called Mälar. "We have fought fierce men and fiercer demons. We fear nothing. We are mortal men, but still men. Speak to us as such or die."

Urd burst into thunderous laughter. His hairy white belly shook up and down. Leaves fluttered in the breeze of his guffaws. Ull said nothing. He gazed down at the mortals with a slight smile.

"You are brave," said Urd. "We shall bear you to the falls. Its location is no secret."

A Skræling arrow zipped through the sky and struck Ull in his cheek. He swatted it from his face with annoyance. A tiny track of blood marked his face. Swiveling his head, he saw the Skræling war party, drawn, no doubt, by Urd's noisy laughter. Ull spun and smashed one hand flat upon the ground. The Earth shook. On the Giant's palm was a bloody goo wrapped in animal skins. He wiped the hand on the top of a nearby tree. No more arrows flew.

Both Giants knelt.

"You are not welcome here," said Urd. "Climb into my hair."

Halberd unbound Labrans but did not release his gag. The brothers climbed up to the Giant's shoulders. They tucked their feet inside the collar of his coarse shirt and wrapped his black hair around their fists, as they would grip the mane of a pony. Usuthu and Mälar climbed aboard Ull and did likewise.

"Beware your brother," called Usuthu.

"What did he say?" asked Urd.

As always, Usuthu had spoken in the language of the Great Steppes. Halberd and Mälar understood him. Halberd hid his surprise at this Immortal who could not understand every mortal tongue.

"He said to beware of my brother, who rides here beside me."

"What's wrong with him?" asked Urd.

"Grettir enchants him. He may slay me."

"And who is Grettir?"

"Grettir is the witch who made a bargain with Thund."

How could this Giant be so ignorant? Was he as stupid as Ragnarok was cunning? Or was his apparent stupidity a clever ruse?

"If he does slay you," said the Giant, with little concern in his deep voice, "my obligation is finished."

The Giants took a few huge steps down the trail. Each time their feet struck the earth a small hole emerged. They gained their speed slowly, like well trained horses. Shortly they were moving in the classic warrior trot. The ground swept by.

Halberd hung on for dear life. The Giants leaped and scrambled. They altered their strides for irregularities in the trail. The ride was not smooth. Trees either tumbled out of the way or huge branches, pushed forward by the Giants, whipped backward at the Northmen on their shoulders.

"Oh, great Urd," asked Halberd, "must you run to the falls? May you not transport us there via a spell?"

"Your presumption is misplaced, mortal," Urd grunted. "We go where we please, by the method which pleases us. We may not and will not share our spells with you."

Halberd said no more. Urd's irritability worried him. Better not to offend the monster.

The ride was rough, but the view was spectacular. Halberd could see from horizon to horizon. The Skrælings were not agricultural and unbroken forest ran as far as he could see. Clear, sparkling lakes and tumbling streams broke the forest here and there.

On the northwest horizon lay a line of odd, spooky mountains unlike any Halberd had seen. Rounded at the top, not pointed, these mountains were covered with trees. No part of the mountains rose above tree line. Their peaks were alternately shrouded in fog and lit by the bright sun. No snow showed on their sides, which were covered with dense evergreen and hardwood trees. If the Giants' course did not change, they would run through the heart of this range.

The trail widened just ahead. Beside the trail stood a huge Skræling village. Longhouses reached beyond the trail into the forest. As the Giants ran, small trees fell over and the longhouses shook. Scores of Eerhahkwoi warriors poured out of their lodges at the warning cries of those in the village. They lined the path, bows at the ready. The Giants ran down the path toward them.

The Skælings stared in wonder. Not one raised his bow. Not one threw a lance. They simply stood by the path, their jaws hanging open, as the Giants ran by.

Three village runners sprinted out of the village after the Giants, but rapidly fell behind and were seen no more.

The Giants reached the mountains by nightfall. Here even Urd and Ull had to climb, and their pace slowed. They crunched trees under their feet. Almost kneeling on the steep, forrested slope, the Giants reached for trees above them. Grabbing those, they pulled themselves up. As often as not, those trees pulled free as the Giants held tight. The Giant's slid back, cursing, and reached up for another handhold. Looking back, Halberd could see a crooked road of destruction cut through the forest.

There will be little difficulty in following our trail, he thought.

Urd went first, yanking trees from the ground and kicking boulders with his huge clumsy feet. Behind him, Ull paid the price. Trees snapped into his face, rocks tumbled against his shins and dirt flew into his eyes.

"Hold, you fat fool," the blonde Giant cried. "I will break trail."

"You shall not," Urd bellowed. "It is my right. I began this journey in front and here I shall stay."

"No," said Ull. The hot tempers of the Giants

flared instantly. In that regard they greatly resembled Dwarfs.

"I believe," spat Urd, "that I am more weary today of your mouth than I was in all the centuries I had to bear your stupid words."

"Trapped in that hump," Ull screeched, "there was little you could do about it. Now you may. Dare you challenge me, you toad?"

Urd slapped Ull full in the face. His quickness was breathtaking. The slap echoed through the mountains. Ull raised one hand to his cheek. He seemed shocked but unhurt.

In that instant Halberd understood whom he had called to his service: Urd's rumbling voice produced thunder and Ull's high voice gave sound to the birds. These were powerful Immortals. They were also, apparently, bitter rivals.

Urd snorted once and turned back up the mountain.

Gasping for breath, Ull reached out and seized Urd by his black hair. He yanked backward. Halberd and Labrans grabbed the collar of Urd's shirt. Though his head snapped, Urd braced himself and did not fall over.

He turned ponderously on the mountain slope and gazed down at Ull. Urd waggled the massive ax in his hand threateningly.

"That was not wise," he said.

"Come, brother," whispered Halberd.

He led Labrans in a fast slide down Urd's shirt sleeve. Urd's fingers nestled in the branches of a tree. Halberd and Labrans hopped from the Giant's hand into the tree.

"Do you like your blonde head on your shoulders, Ull?" spat Urd. "Or would you rather see it bouncing down among these trees?"

Ull pulled his dagger out of his sheath with a sweeping flourish. Halberd could not see Usuthu or Mälar. Halberd heard a rustle in the tree beside him. Peering through the moonlight, Halberd saw Labrans climbing down the tree. He was trying to escape. Halberd slid down the rough trunk. Skin flew from his hands and stayed on the tree. He laid his sword point gently onto Labrans' hand.

His brother looked from his hand to Halberd's face. Halberd shook his head and gestured to the top of the tree. Labrans climbed back up.

"You owe me a vow," Halberd screamed at the Giants. "You have sworn to carry me to the falls."

Urd barely turned his head.

"I shall carry you, mortal, when I have dispatched this pretty fool."

Mälar's voice rang out of the forest: "I thought you were allies," he called, "or friends."

"Friends?" snorted Ull, "With this clumsy behemoth, this cow?"

Ull wove his dagger back and forth.

Urd swung his ax overhead. Ull stepped aside. The mammoth blade sank to the handle into the ground. Urd pulled on it once as Ull slashed at his arms.

Urd jumped down the hill and grappled with Ull. As they tumbled, trees broke in their path as blades of grass fall when two children wrestle in a field. The earth shook as they rolled. The trees swayed back and forth. Halberd held the trunk with one hand and his sword point on his brother's back with the other.

When the tree stopped moving, Halberd looked down the hill. Ull's dagger flashed through the night. Urd fell backward.

Ull straddled Urd, who lay on his back amid a forest of broken trees. Ull reversed his grip and raised the dagger over his head. He smiled from ear to ear. Then he raised the dagger higher and bent to slam it home.

Urd's sword drove into the junction of his legs. The blonde Giant raised his head and screamed in his high, broken voice. Birds broke from all the trees at the sound and wheeled into the night. The point of the sword burst through Ull's colored robe and thrust toward the moon.

Ull went to his knees. He opened his mouth to scream and a small river of blood poured out. The sword butt was wedged against a broken tree. Ull could not move it.

Urd slid from beneath him. His red shirt was black with Ull's blood. He bore a dagger cut across his throat. It bled but a trickle. Urd worked his ax free from the ground. He stood behind Ull and raised the ax high with a twist of his body.

He uncoiled slowly and rested his ax. Smiling viciously, Urd reached out. He took the tip of the sword in his hand. Its point was slippery with Ull's blood and small clots of flesh.

"Tell me, Ull?" Urd asked in his low, rumbling

voice, "does this cause you pain?" Urd shook the sword point like a dog shaking a rat.

Ull's whimpers would have been terrible to hear in a man. Coming from a Giant, especially one of such noble bearing, they were unbearable.

"Grant him mercy, Urd," called Mälar. "Kill him and be done with it."

"Silence, mortal. Or do you wish to be my dinner?" Urd rooted among the broken trees until he found Ull's dagger. Ull knelt in a small pond of his own blood. Urd touched Ull on the surface of one eye with the dagger. Ull shook once more. Urd twisted the knife and Ull's eye popped out of his head. It fell down his chest, dangling as Hel's had dangled. Ull's voice gurgled in his chest as he choked on his own blood.

"Enough," came the calm, steady voice.

Urd turned, the glistening dagger in his hands. Clear liquid dripped from its huge point.

"Who speaks?" he bellowed.

"Usuthu of the Great Steppes," came the reply, "mortal and archer. If you do not pick up your ax and give your brother a warrior's death, I shall blind you where you stand."

"What language is that?" bellowed Urd. "I do not understand what this large black mortal says."

"He says," spoke Mälar with dignity, "that you should grant your fellow Giant a merciful death immediately or face the consequences."

"Bah!"

Urd turned back to Ull, the dagger outstretched. Something whooshed in the night sky. Urd's left

eye burst. Blood and clear fluid ran down his cheek.
He went to his knees beside Ull, sobbing like a
child.

"I know you will recover from this wound," said
Usuthu over the sound of Urd's sobs and Ull's
dying, choking breaths. "I am mortal and you are a
Giant. But great pain will I cause you unless you do
my bidding. Slay Ull."

Urd rose unsteadily to his feet. He raised his ax
and rotated his body away from Ull. Urd uncoiled
from the waist, turning rapidly and developing
speed. The ax blade whistled. It launched Ull's
head from his shoulders and slipped from Urd's
blood-slick hands. The bleeding blonde head and
the bloody ax sailed through the sky. The bleeding
head, trailing a comet of blonde curls, hit first,
clipping the tops of trees and bouncing out of sight.
The ax simply disappeared, smashing into a forest
and crashing into the ground.

Growls sounded from near the head. Great bears
were coming up from underground to feed on the
Giant's flesh. Urd stood wheezing and weeping,
cupping his exploded eye in his hand. Halberd motioned Labrans to follow him.

He slid down the tree. When Labrans touched
the ground, Halberd shoved him off his feet. He
quickly bound Labrans hand and foot, cutting bloody
strips from Ull's robe to do the job. When Labrans
was secured, Halberd strode quickly to Urd's feet.

Halberd drew Hrungnir and slammed the point
into Urd's ankle. The Giant screamed and tried to
snatch his leg away, but Halberd held fast. Urd

could not move the foot. Hrungnir held him in check.

"I command you now, you fat murdering idiot, to take us to the Thundering Falls. That is your vow, your oath and your duty. Until you fulfill this vow, you are mine to command."

Urd nodded his head. He stuck Ull's dagger into his belt and bent at the waist. He reached toward Ull.

Halberd shook Hrungnir as Urd had shaken Ull. Urd gasped.

"What do you want?" asked Halberd.

"His sword," the Giant replied through gritted teeth.

"You may not have it. You do not need it. Pick my brothers up gently."

Usuthu and Mälar emerged from the devastated woods. Urd lowered a hand. Usuthu and Mälar ran onto his blood-encrusted palm. Usuthu kept his bow drawn tightly. His arrow never wavered from Urd's eye, even as Urd lifted them in his open palm to his shoulder. Usuthu sprang from Urd's hand. He ran along his shoulder. Ducking his head, Usuthu ran into one of Urd's huge ears. He scratched the Giant once, from the inside, with the point of his arrow.

"If you wish to die," the Mongol called in a muffled voice, "then fail to do my brother's bidding."

"Pick up Labrans from the base of this tree," Halberd said.

"Who," asked the Giant, "is Labrans?"

"He is my brother who lays bound at the foot of this tree, you brutal oaf! Pick him up."

Urd raised Labrans to his shoulder. Mälar guided Labrans into a sitting position and unbound his hands. He then bound Labrans into Urd's hair. Halberd pulled Hrungnir from the Giant's ankle.

"Now me," he said.

When Halberd was on Urd's shoulder, he placed the point of Hrungnir on the back of Urd's neck.

"Defy me once, you fool," he said, "and I will kill you. Now move."

Urd started west once more. He did not trot. He shambled along, fighting for balance and holding one hand over his eye.

Urd ceased weeping. As the night wore on his speed increased. They ran through the mountains and back into a forested plain. Urd splashed through streams that reached his knees and small rivers that he either leapt in a bound or slogged through doggedly, the water coming up to his waist.

Dawn brought them to the edge of a great river. Halberd could see to the other side, but it was formidable nonetheless. Urd waded in without stopping. The water passed his knees, then his waist, rose to his chest and came near his shoulders. Still he waded on.

"Hold, Urd," commanded Halberd.

The Giant stopped. The frigid water lapped at Halberd's feet.

"We are not so apparently stupid as the Giants

think," Halberd said. "You will not drown us. Are you able to swim?"

Urd nodded his head without speaking.

"Then wait until I give you the signal. Will you swim on your chest or your back?"

Urd shook his head irritably. He did not reply.

"I shall choose for you," Halberd said. "We shall ride in your hair and you shall swim on your chest. If you roll over, duck your head or so much as splash us, I will assume you are trying to drown me and I will break your skull with my sacred knife. Now, you sack of dung, nod your head that you understand me."

Urd nodded.

Halberd called Usuthu out of the Giant's ear. They wove their hands into Urd's hair and braced their feet on his skull. Using his hair as ropes, they climbed to the top of his head. Halberd wrapped Urd's hair around each of them, binding the black strands into thick knots. When all were safe, Halberd tapped the Giant on the head with the point of his knife.

Urd eased himself into the river and swam easily. The fat Giant carried his head high out of the water and kicked his legs like a frog. His arms drew a circle under the water. They moved rapidly across the river.

"Why do they feud so?" said Usuthu. "Since they were trapped in the Dwarf's hump together I assumed they were close allies."

"So did I," said Halberd, "but now we see

that Giants vary in their nature as wildly as humans. Ragnarok was brave and capable of humor. Of Ull we know nothing, except that he fought poorly. Urd is a snake, without loyalty or even cunning. He will try to kill us when his vow is fulfilled."

"Can we actually slay him?" asked Mälar.

"I can kill him with Hrungnir. Usuthu's arrows are large enough to cause him pain. I pray it does not come to that."

"There are other, fouler deaths for a sheep gelder like him," Usuthu said darkly. "He slays without reason or merit. He enjoys torture. Immortal or not, he is an animal."

"What do you mean?"

"I will not say. If he trifles with us further, do not reach for Hrungnir immediately. I will teach this murderer what blood sport is all about."

Usuthu looked away. His jaw was set. He would say no more.

Mälar and Halberd shrugged at each other.

"My brother, do what you must," Halberd said. "After what we have seen in this world I feel nothing could surprise me."

Urd shot sideways in the river, flailing his arms in front of him. The Northmen and the Mongol were doused. Halberd raised Hrungnir.

"If I kill him, Usuthu," he said, "just fall into the water and roll onto your back. We will save you."

Usuthu nodded.

"Hold, Urd," Mälar called, "what are you doing?"

Urd raised his head.

"A fiendish serpent," he cried. "She struck me and vanished under the water."

"Swim, Giant," ordered Halberd. "If Niddhog swims in fresh water as easily as the great salt oceans we may well be finished."

Urd kicked his feet harder and pulled with his hands. A wall of water swept up over his massive forehead and drenched his passengers. They clung to his hair and stood on his head, scanning the river for the serpent. They saw nothing.

Urd stood and slogged toward shore. The water level fell away quickly. It dropped to his chest, then his hips, then his thighs. He took one more step. Urd pitched flat onto his face. Halberd, Mälar, Usuthu and Labrans flew off his head and tumbled into the shallows with a rolling splash.

Something unseen dragged Urd back into the river. The Giant struck at his foot with Ull's dagger. Still he traveled backward. He sank into the river to his neck. Water filled his mouth. Urd shoved the dagger into dirt at the river's edge and hung on. Still, he could not resist whatever yanked him. Blood rose to the surface.

"Save me, Halberd," he called.

"Usuthu," said Halberd, "if you have a strategy against this unseen demon, use it. I care not for this fool's life, but I dread the walk that lies ahead."

Usuthu stepped into the river to his ankles. He pulled the silver mallet from around his neck and held it to the cloudless dawn.

"O Great Wotan," he called in a singsong voice,

"save this murdering Giant for our immediate purposes. He is evil and should die, but we are mortals and require his aid. I swear to you, Wotan, in the name of your master, Bahaab Dahaabs, that I will not permit him to go unpunished."

The wind rose along the riverbank. Waves appeared on the water. A black cloud formed on the horizon and swept toward them.

"I do not, O Wotan, ask that you slay whatever beast attacks this Giant. Only that you separate him from his prey, that we might force the Giant to fulfill his vow to us, your unworthy servants."

"This beast," whispered Mälar into Halberd's ear, "must not be too hungry. The long-winded nature of Usuthu's magic would give him time to devour the Giant whole and pick his teeth besides."

Urd screamed with pain through the water in his mouth. More blood bubbled to the surface. Urd would not let go of the bank to attack his attacker. The black cloud grew overhead and soared down the bank. It held no blue or silver, as most thunder clouds do. It was pure, impenetrable black.

Usuthu stood unmoving, his tiny mallet held to the darkening sky. The single black cloud stopped overhead. It blotted out the sun. A chill wind swept across the river. White waves broke on the shore. The river exploded upward. A geyser shot straight up until it touched the cloud.

For one brief instant an apparition appeared. Niddhog, lacking three toes on one rear foot, blood and flesh in his claws, hung frozen in the blue sky between the roiling river and the black cloud. The dragon seemed to stop in midair, not moving, not breathing, neither rising toward the cloud nor falling to the water: frozen in time and space.

The cloud raced back down the river. The wind dropped. The swells sank back into the ocean. The sun shone brightly with the warmth of a spring dawn. Morning birds called from the trees.

Usuthu hung the mallet around his neck.

"Thank you, Wotan, Master of this World."

Halberd and Mälar looked to the Giant.

Urd dragged himself along the riverbank onto the dirt. His left leg was raked with claw marks from knee to foot. Every inch of skin had been clawed off. Flesh hung in symmetrical strips. No bones showed and the damage was not severe. The pain, however, must have been intense. The scars from this attack would last a lifetime, perhaps even an eternity.

"What make you of this assault?" Mälar asked Halberd as the Giant sat whimpering on the riverbank, his hairy, sagging belly protruding from his blood-stained shirt.

"Hel sends a clear warning: She could have killed us, but she chose to attack the Giant. His wounds are meaningless but dramatic. By this message she instructs all other Giants and Dwarfs to spurn our calls for aid. Niddhog did not try to kill the Giant, but to maim him and cause him pain. Urd will blabber this to all who dwell in Midgard."

"He will deliver a different message when he

gets home," said Usuthu. "He will fear us more than any serpent."

"Further," Halberd continued, "Hel tells us that she knows where we are, that she stalks us and that she will have her way with us when she chooses."

"Only" answered Mälar, "she will not."

"If her father elects to help her, we are doomed."

"That is true of all men in all lands, Halberd," snapped Mälar. "If a particular God turns his wrath on a particular mortal, that mortal will not survive. If Loki so chooses we are powerless. I will not concern myself until it occurs."

Halberd strode to Urd and put Hrungnir against his massive neck.

"Stop your whining, you dog," Halberd said. "Rise to your feet and bear us west."

Wiping his tears with a hairy forearm, Urd struggled to his knees. He plucked his dagger from the riverbank and looked, for a moment, at the mortals. Usuthu stood in ankle-deep water, his arrow scant feet from the Giant's eye.

"Do it," the Mongol said.

Urd needed no translation. Usuthu's intention was clear.

Urd sheathed his dagger and stood gingerly. He tromped around the water's edge, testing his ankle and blowing his nose through his fingers.

"What is it about his cowardice that arouses my anger so?" Halberd asked Mälar.

"He is a bully," answered the navigator. "He possesses outer strength but no strength of character."

"He deserves a bully's fate," Halberd said.

"Never fear," called Usuthu, "he shall have it."

Urd knelt and extended one hand upon the shore. They walked up his arm carefully, leading the bound Labrans. All settled into the giant's collar once more.

"He stinks," Usuthu said.

"His bath did him little good," answered Mälar.

"He doesn't stink of sweat," Usuthu said contemptously. "He stinks of fear. An Immortal who fears so deeply; it is shameful."

Urd set off, running north up the bank of the big river. They ran past villages of Skræling fishermen. Canoes filled the rivers and nets dried on the shore. After some time, when the sun was at high noon, they turned west once more, along the banks of a smaller, fast-moving river.

The countryside opened up. They ran in the middle of a long valley. The valley was split in two by the river that Urd followed. Far to the south and closer to the north, scattered small mountains rose from the forest. These did not seem to be ranges but instead random mountains without pattern. Like the larger mountains to the east, these were rounded and covered with trees.

The trees were no longer predominately evergreen. Hardwoods filled the rolling hills. Urd ran easily along the valley. His scarred leg posed no apparent problem. Occasionally he would slow at a small spring-fed lake and dunk his bad leg in to the knee.

"Remember these springs, mortal," Urd said. "Their waters have the power to heal."

The river petered out late in the day. The valley opened and the rolling hills became flatter and flatter. In place of the river were many small lakes, similar in shape, each roughly a league wide and several leagues long. Skræling villages dotted the lakeshore. As he neared the first of these lakes, Urd spoke over his shoulder. "Climb into my hair and bind yourself. These lakes are too deep to walk. I shall swim."

True to his word, the Giant plunged into each lake with a huge splash. The clear, cold water soaked his passengers, but caused him little reason to slow down. Urd swam swiftly. Whether he was gaining strength as the journey went on, or his fear of Niddhog drove him like a lash, Halberd could not say.

The Northmen did little talking. Usuthu dozed with one hand wrapped in the Giant's hair. Labrans watched every mile of ground with care, as if memorizing his route home. Mälar did the same. He scanned the horizon for landmarks and carefully calculated the distance they had traveled. Mälar noted where the sun stood in relation to the mountains to the south and north. He measured with his practiced eye the leagues between the collection of finger-shaped lakes and the rolling plains that lay before them to the west.

Halberd looked all the while to the west, one hand holding Urd's shirt and the other resting Hrungnir lightly on the Giant's neck. Halberd thought briefly about Usuthu. The Mongol never boasted or made threats, yet he prophesied the death of the Giant every time he opened his mouth. The Giant's repulsive conduct had deeply offended the Mongol. If he said Urd would pay, then payment was forthcoming.

Urd alternated between swimming and running until well past dusk. When the last of the lakes vanished behind them, the land grew even flatter. Urd loped easily, eating up ground. He ran all night through heavy woods and flat terrain. As dawn neared, the roar of a great, swift river could be faintly heard.

They gained the riverbanks as the sun rose. The river was vast. The opposite bank stood several leagues away. A huge island, more than twenty leagues long, split the river in twain. On the shore of the island stood a cluster of cone-shaped Skrælings tents. Several canoes were drawn up onto the beach.

Urd rested on its bank, sitting in the mud and extending his vast legs into the water. He splashed happily, like a small boy. He scooped water into his virtually toothless mouth and spat it high into the air. The spray lit up the sky with a series of tiny rainbows.

"I am not sorry to stop," Halberd said, dunking himself in the river and wringing the dirt from his clothes.

"Nor I," said Mälar, "but this river bothers me. There is something odd about it, something I have seldom seen."

"You grow blind, old man," laughed Usuthu. "This river is odd because it flows to the north."

"And we approach it from the south and the

east," said Mälar in wonder. "Urd," he called, "does this mean that the Thundering Falls flows to the north?"

"Aye," answered the Giant irritably, "what difference does it make?"

"Have you seen the falls?"

"Often."

"And the Lakes Which You May Not See Across?"

"Those too." Urd rolled onto his stomach and rested his head in his hands as he answered Mälar. He lightly kicked the tips of his toes in the river. He seemed harmless as a pup.

"How many are there? What are they like?"

"Well, mortal," Urd answered, "there are six or seven, I cannot remember clearly. They mostly lie east-west and they are vast. No freshwater lakes like them exist in your world, of which I am aware. The falls flows north into one of them, via a raging river and a deep, narrow gorge. The inhabitants of this land know the lakes well."

"At the falls," Halberd asked, "do you know exactly where you're taking us?"

"There is a cave hidden beneath the falls. It lies at the conjunction of important lines of power that course through the Earth. It is a potent spot."

"Let us make for it, then," Usuthu said shortly.

Urd rolled onto his haunches and lowered a hand. Usuthu nocked an arrow and aimed into the Giant's eye. Halberd, Mälar and Labrans climbed to their perch. Usuthu followed.

The Giant trotted up the bank of the river. A distant drumming grew louder. The drumming became a pounding as they moved north and the pounding slowly evolved into thunder. The thunder built in volume until nothing else could be heard.

Halberd looked around, as did Mälar. No falls were visible. Only the river, moving faster than any water Halberd had seen. The rapids were intense, but Halberd was accustomed to boiling rapids. He was accustomed to narrow rivers that shot through tight valleys. Never had he seen so broad a river move with such force.

Urd reached the end of the riverbank. Ahead was a sheer cliff. The thunder roared. Mist sprayed far into the air.

"Where are the falls?" Mälar screamed into Urd's ear.

Urd pointed.

They could see the huge river disappear over a cliff edge, but no more. A stone island split the river just before the water plummeted over. The entire width of the river slid over this edge, but the other side was concealed from view.

"The climb is treacherous," Urd shouted in his booming, rumbling voice. The mist bathed his face. "Cling to me tightly or die. I will not concern myself with you as I climb."

"Hold, then, for a moment," Halberd yelled in reply.

Halberd slit the edge of Urd's filthy, wet shirt just outside the collar. Using unraveling thread from the shirt, which was as rope to the mortals, Halberd lashed each person to the shirt. All wove strands of Urd's hair tightly around them.

Halberd poked Urd in the back of the head. Urd slid to the cliff edge.

Halberd could not see beyond the thick black hair in front of his face. The Thundering Falls beat about his head. The sound of the falls and the power of its strength filled his heart with joyous rapture. This was the kernel of adventure. Northmen sailed the world to touch the pulse of existence, to know that they lived, proud and mobile, while farmers rotted and kings died of boredom. Here was the essence of freedom, the essence of life. Halberd knew they had reached a place of great, great power.

The mist enveloped them, soaking them to the skin. The falls could grow no louder; their ears could accept no more volume. But through skin, muscles and nerve, Halberd felt the falls grow more intense.

All movement stopped.

"Open your eyes, mortals," Urd called, even his voice full of joy, "we have reached the bottom."

Urd curled one hand around to his shoulder. Halberd and his men untied and clambered onto his hand. Urd raised the hand high above his head. His face was split by a huge grin. The power of the falls thundered through him, as it did through all of them.

When his arm was extended as far above his head as it would go, Urd opened his fingers. Halberd was high, high, above the base of the falls.

Above him, shooting over the precipice and tumbling down, was an immense, immeasurable wall of water. It poured over the cliff sparkling white, full of rainbows and reflections as brilliant as diamonds. The water fell into a vast lagoon and rebounded up half the height of the falls itself. The falling water mingled with the rising water until it was impossible to tell which was which.

Below the falls to the north was a boiling cataract of swirling currents and choppy white-water rapids, each churning pool as large as some of the lakes Urd had swam across.

Those rapids plunged down through a narrow gorge that ran for leagues north of the falls. The racing water threw giant spumes of white over the walls of the gorge. Its brown rock walls were drenched. The ground above the gorge was a sea of mud.

Urd lowered them to his shoulder. His eyes were bright with excitement. His breath came short. He panted like a dog, breathing through his mouth in explosive grunts.

The Northmen clustered around one huge ear. Urd pointed into the heart of the falls.

"I shall climb to the base of the falls," he yelled, "Circle around the curtain of water on the bordering rocks and then climb the cliff wall you cannot now see. The falling water hides it. Inside that cliff is a cave. It is the seat of all the falls' power. In it is fresh water and dry shelter. Also, much firewood. The Giants and Dwarfs use it often."

"Will we be alone there?" Halberd shouted into the flapping ear.

Urd nodded. "I am the only one of my people in this place at this time."

"Go to, then," called Mälar.

They tied themselves down as before. The Falls beat in their chests like another heart.

Urd picked his way carefully among the slick, black, shiny rocks. The water boiled white and gray at his feet. The falls fell directly overhead. Urd moved to the far edge of the white curtain of water. Here, the rising mist obscured everything. Urd gripped the black rocks and climbed a short distance up the cliff wall. A quick sideways hop carried him around a vertical knife-edge of sheer rock.

The sound of the falls changed. They were no longer in front of it. The mists vanished. They looked up. Towering over them was a sheer wall of black rock dripping with moss and trickles of clear, cold water. Halfway up were a series of large cave mouths. In front of the cliff fell an unbelieveable wall of green water. They gazed at the Thundering Falls from behind.

Urd mounted the cliff and climbed with great care. He passed several caves. His head drew even with the mouth of the largest one, which appeared big enough for the Giant to enter. With a shrug of his shoulder he gestured for his passengers to dismount. They scrambled into the cave.

A few feet back from the entrance the cave was remarkably dry. And vast.

The rock ceiling towered overhead, high enough

for Urd to have stood on the shoulders of Ull and still not bumped his head. They could not see the back of the cave. The rear half of the cave floor appeared to be dirt, which would mean comfortable sleeping. A gurgle, barely audible over the constant din of the falls, told them that clean water ran through their shelter.

Against one wall ran a stack of firewood on a scale with the falls itself. The chopped wood reached to the roof of the cave and disappeared into the halflight at the rear wall. A cookfire pit, lined with stones, marked the center of the cave.

"An ox could roast in that pit," said Halberd.

"Or three villages," answered Mälar.

Labrans stumbled to the stream running through the cave. Urd swung his huge legs into the entrance. Halberd followed Labrans and cut his hands free and removed his gag.

"Drink, brother," he said.

Usuthu and Mälar made room for Urd at the entrance. The Giant blocked most of the light.

"Urd," said Usuthu, "why here?"

"Because," the Giant said, drawing his dagger as he smiled with bright, bright eyes, "this is where Grettir bade me bring you. I fulfilled my vow to Halberd and my bargain with the witch. You are here safely, as I vowed. And soon to this cave will come Grettir and her Skræling host.

"First, however, I will have my revenge on you, black mortal. Your insolent threats have pounded into my head these many days. Now you shall pay."

Urd reached for Usuthu. He underestimated the

Mongol's quickness. Usuthu leaped aside. Mälar brought the ax crashing down into the Giant's hand. The first knuckle on his first finger fell free, blood sending it on its way. Mälar kicked the first joint out of the cave. It tumbled through the clear light that shined through the falls and vanished into the mist below.

Urd swung backhanded at Mälar, but the navigator sprang onto the Giant's arm, slashed at the vein in his wrist, and leapt off the other side.

Halberd drew Hrungnir and rushed forward.

"Hold!"

The power of command rang through Usuthu's voice. All froze. The falls pounded on.

Usuthu held the silver mallet overhead.

"Urd," he pronounced deliberately, "you are a traitor, a murderer, a fool and a miserable warrior. You deserve to die but I shall not kill you. Worse, I shall humiliate you forever."

Urd appeared trapped and puzzled. He scraped the dagger blade sideways across the cave floor, throwing sparks over Usuthu's head. Usuthu jumped the blade easily, though it was half his height.

Usuthu landed running. He dashed at the Giant, who knelt on the cave floor. Urd did not seem to accept that he was in danger.

"By the power of Bahaad Dahaabs, I cripple you for your immortal life!"

Usuthu smashed the mallet into Urd's outer thigh just above the knee. It was the highest point on the kneeling Giant's leg that Usuthu could reach.

A sickening, splintering crack accompanied the

raw white shard of bone that burst through Urd's ragged leggings. Urd squealed like a pig and grabbed his leg. His forgotten dagger rang off the stone entrance to the cave and plummetted into the lagoon far, far below. The golden handle threw reflected beams of light into the constant wall of falling water. A succession of rainbows followed the huge knife as it fell. Its splash reached nearly to the mouth of the cave.

Usuthu stepped forward again and swung the mallet at Urd's wrist. Again the horrible crack sounded and Urd's huge hand fell open. His fingers twitched spasmodically. The large bone of his forearm stuck through the red cloth of his shirt at a repulsive angle. Blood welled up at the sleeve and dripped from the end of the white, white bone.

Usuthu ran right over the broken wrist, up the frozen Giant's arm and along his shoulder. He raised his mallet.

"For the needlessly murdered Ull," the Mongol cried, "perhaps your friend, perhaps not, I do not care!"

Usuthu drove the hammer straight into the black center of Urd's eye. The eye exploded, spurting fluid and bright blue blood across the cave. Urd screamed in agony and raised his good hand to his eye. As he did, he leaned back out over the cave mouth. He shot his other hand out to seize the cave wall, but his broken wrist would not answer him. Urd's strengthless fingernails scrabbled on the wet rock.

His back arched. He hung halfway out the cave,

fighting for balance. Then he slipped from the cave mouth as slowly as a snail moving down a stone fence. Inch by inch he slipped, one huge hairy hand covering his ruined eye, one flopping, broken hand desperately trying for purchase. Urd would not uncover his eye to grab with his good hand and his broken hand could not grip.

Halberd, Usuthu and Mälar watched in silent awe as the Giant went off the cliff. He turned slightly in midair and his hands fell from his face. His slack jaw hit the water first. His widespread arms followed. The boiling pool swallowed the Giant without a trace.

The last sight they had of Urd was the soles of his big ugly feet.

An explosion of water splashed back over their heads. They raced for the back of the cave, but not in time. A solid wall of green swept into the cave mouth, picked them up like dolls and slammed them into the far wall. The huge wave ran back out the cave mouth, leaving small pools and eddies behind.

Labrans' Last Words

Halberd raised his head. It was difficult, because he seemed to be sitting on it. His chest and legs were above him, plastered to the cave wall by the splash. He tucked his hands under his head and somersaulted off the wall onto his feet.

Usuthu knelt on his hands and knees, slowly lowering the silver mallet over his head and around his neck. His shields were bent and marked by stones. His knees and elbows bled. His forehead was gashed. Mud covered him. Mälar already sat in the spring, splashing the mud from his tunic and shaking moss and clumps of dirt from his hair.

Labrans rested his back against the wall, his legs splayed slack in front of him and his mouth hanging open. He appeared dazed. When Halberd stood, he realized he was drenched in mud. He splashed into the spring and washed himself, scrubbing harshly.

"Now we know," said Mälar, grinning through the blood running from his split lip.

"Know what?" Halberd asked, with an inward

sigh. There was no end to the old man's high spirits.

"Know whether Urd was cunning or stupid. He was both, cunning enough to deposit us in a trap and stupid enough to say so."

"We must barricade the cave entrance, "Usuthu said, "and prepare for siege."

"Why bother?" asked Mälar. "We have a supreme defensive position. They cannot climb up here without exposing themselves. We could not be safer."

"Did you see the cliffs above us?" Halberd snapped. "They are honeycombed with caves. The Eerhahkwoi might be there already. Grettir may be able to transport her warriors through solid matter. We might be attacked through the rock walls of this cave."

"Precisely my point," Mälar said triumphantly. "If she might attack from any direction why should we bother building any defense? We should sharpen our swords and wait for the battle."

"I believe you are tired from your long ride and wish to sleep," said Halberd. "So be it. Usuthu and I will take the first watch. You sleep."

"Very well," answered Mälar. He slopped through the mud at the rear of the cave and climbed the high wall of firewood. At its top he curled himself to fit the irregular lines of logs. In a moment he snored.

Labrans had not moved. His chest swelled with even breathing, so he was not dead.

Halberd and Usuthu ignored him. They moved swiftly to the forward end of the log pile. Halberd unclasped his chest armor. He rested his armor and sword on the rocky floor. He climbed to the top of the pile and began to throw logs to Usuthu. The logs that Halberd required three motions to pitch below, Usuthu gathered in one armful. They swiftly built a low wall along the mouth of the huge cave. As Mälar snored the wall slowly grew. After a few hours it reached as high as Halberd's shoulders.

The sky darkened.

"Grettir might prefer to wait for nightfall," Halberd said, "but the Skrælings are savages. Savages do not like to fight at night."

"No one," said Usuthu, "could climb that wet wall in the dark of night. Their assault will come at twilight or dawn, but at no time in between."

"Then you watch the walls until sundown and I'll build a fire."

Halberd walked to the rear of the cave. Labrans lay in the mud, hugging himself in sleep like a baby. Mud filled his ears and coated his head. His clothing was soaked. Halberd hefted logs into the cook-fire pit and built a roaring blaze. Its flames reached high above his head and threw flickering shadows on the vast cave walls. The feeling of great power and joy had not deserted Halberd. Even these simple chores filled him with gladness. The energy of the Thundering Falls pumped through him. Truly this was a magical place.

Halberd roused Labrans and led him to the fire. Labrans did not focus his eyes or speak. He shook, as with uncontrollable fever. The fire did not seem to warm him.

Halberd went back to the cave mouth. Usuthu sat

at its edge, in front of the defensive wall, his legs dangling over the raging rapids below. His bow rested beside him. The falls drummed on, a silver-green wall almost near enough to touch. The sky was a rich golden-purple. Not many minutes of daylight remained.

"What have you seen?" Halberd asked him, hypnotized by the falls.

"A Skræling," Usuthu answered calmly, "has been climbing this wall as the sun sets. He is halfway up. Soon he will reach our cave, if he does not follow Urd into the rapids."

"Has he seen you? How can you be so calm?"

"We only saw this cave because Urd, that foul hog, raised us on his palm. The wall is too sheer and high. No one below may see this cave. But I think he knows where it is. I do not believe he knows we await him."

"Why?"

"He moves without caution. He is lightly armed. I believe he is a scout."

"Can you see the main force?"

"I'm not certain the larger group is nearby. If this Skræling is enchanted like Labrans, Grettir will read the situation through his eyes. Then she can decide how to proceed without any threat to her army."

Halberd climbed the log pile and awoke Mälar. The old man swung nimbly to the fire and turned his back to it gratefully. Labrans took no notice of either of them.

"I've been wet for three days," Mälar said. "It feels good to be dry."

"Arm yourself, navigator. A Skræling scout climbs this cliff."

Mälar sauntered casually to the log wall. He would not step beyond its edge to look down. He lay his quiver on the cave floor and beckoned Halberd.

"Give me your bow and arrows," he said. "Enough space remains between this wall and the cliff edge to grant our enemies a moment to charge us. I wish to establish my position."

"What of your lust for my ax?"

"By the time I need the ax I will be dead. But leave it beside me all the same."

Halberd climbed over the log wall.

"He is just below us," Usuthu whispered, waving Halberd backward with an open hand. "Do not speak."

One brown hand appeared over the cliff edge. Halberd and Usuthu flattened themselves against the wall of the entrance. A grunting breath preceded the Skræling's head. He was an Eerhahkwoi; his long hair hung in braids, and a thin ruff of hair stood straight up in the middle. He wore soft skin leggings and no shirt. Around his chest he bore a crudely plaited rope, obviously of Northland design.

He levered one knee onto the cave mouth and wrenched himself to his feet. He was lean and strong. A stone knife hung from his belt and a stone-headed chopping hatchet dangled on a line behind him. Despite his climb, he was not breathing hard.

The sun had set. Long rosy fingers crossed the sky, but light was fading. The inside of the cave was pure dark. The Skræling took a cautious step forward, one hand over his brow.

Labrans screamed a warning in the Skræling tongue. The warrior raised his hatchet as Labrans jumped from the fire and raced toward the log wall. Mälar yanked him down and the two wrestled noisily across the cave floor.

Labrans had apparently screamed for help. The Skræling made for the wall, his hatchet upraised. Usuthu reached out of the shadows and grabbed the Skræling by his wrist. As the shocked Eerhahkwoi swung his head to see his attacker. Usuthu lifted him off his feet and cracked him like a whip, pivoting the Eerhahkwoi by his arm and snapping him head-on into the rock wall. The Skræling's breath fled with an explosive whump! He fell back onto the floor, blood pouring from his face.

"Did you kill him?"

"I broke only his nose, not his head," Usuthu replied.

Usuthu bent over and took the Skræling by his hair.

"What," asked Halberd, "are you doing?"

"I doubt that I can fling this warrior the entire distance to the Beach of Blood, but I shall attempt it. Our current vantage gives me sufficient height to warrant the effort."

"Bind him for me, brother," Halberd said quietly. "We can use this warrior, and we shall. Labrans will speak what his mistress has taught him."

Labran's demonic grace and speed kept Mälar at bay. Labrans had Halberd's ax. He cut at the navigator with wild, wide whooshing swings. Mälar dared not draw near.

Halberd approached his brother as one would a crazed animal in a trap. He circled well to Labrans' right. Mälar moved to his left. Labrans held the ax upright, swiveling his head from one to the other.

"Lower the ax," Halberd said quietly. "I need your help, brother. Come and give your fellow adventurers aid."

"I'll aid my mistress by slicing off your head," Labrans cackled. Foam formed at the corners of his mouth. He turned to Halberd.

"Step closer, younger brother," he yelped. "Let me make your former lover happy. Let me kill you."

The ax dropped. Labrans' head fell to his chest. He keeled over, his limbs absolutely without strength. The rock that Mälar had bounced off his head chunked into the floor.

"Quickly," Halberd said. "Use the Skræling's rope and bind them back-to-back."

The deed was soon done. The Eerhahkwoi and Labrans sat near the fire, tied back-to-back, their arms bound inside the thick plaited line. Halberd stood over Labrans, the jewel and Hrungnir almost touching. The veins in Halberd's arms popped from the effort of pushing them together. When they almost touched, Halberd nodded to Mälar.

Mälar flung water into Labrans' face. Labrans shook his head sullenly. He looked up at Halberd.

"I despise you," he whispered.

209

The hatred in his face and voice broke Halberd's heart. Was this creature his own blood? Was Grettir so strong?

"Hrungnir and Jewel of Kyrwyn-Coyne," Halberd called, his voice booming through the vast cavern. "Combat the spell that enslaves my poor brother! Turn him to my use. Let him translate the speech of this brave Skræling scout. If in his heart there beats one drop of love for his brother, Halberd, let him resist the witch!"

The jewel and the knife sprang from Halberd's hands. Bound by unseen ties, locked together yet not touching, spinning slowly in the flickering firelight, the jewel and the knife rose to the top of the cave and slowly lowered, their golden glow spreading.

Halberd stood aside. The implements lowered to Labrans' head. They slowly revolved above him. Their glow lit the cave brighter than firelight. Mälar averted his eyes from the glare. Usuthu watched carefully, as if memorizing the ceremony.

The Skræling's eyes rolled back in his head with fear. He sobbed in terror. No tears fell. He certainly did not know he made such sounds.

Even Halberd felt some fear; he was unleashing potent forces. If Grettir controlled Labrans she might use him to modify this spell.

The glow spread over Labrans, carefully outlining him as it had Halberd. The knife and the jewel hovered over him. Labrans' arms, legs and head glowed golden and his face became serene.

"Ask him," Halberd spoke in a breathless whisper, "his name."

Labrans coughed out a question in the gutteral clicking tongue.

The reply was brief. Following the words was an ocean of vomit. The Skræling's fear overwhelmed his body. He gasped his food out over his skin leggings. When the racking coughs left his body, he looked up at his captors, shame blazing in his face.

"No one outside his tribe," spoke Labrans, "not even Grettir, has ever spoken his tongue aloud. He is deeply fearful."

"How does she communicate with them?"

Another fast exchange in the rattling, coughing language filled the flickering cave. Halberd, Mälar and Usuthu stood rapt, not daring to breathe.

"Her voice," said Labrans, "sounds in their heads. Her lips never move."

"May the Gods," whispered Mälar, "help us now. There is no escaping her."

"Demand," said Halberd, "that he tell us his name."

"His name," answered Labrans, speaking without emotion, "is Two Dogs."

Mälar burst out laughing. He rolled onto his back and drummed his heels on the floor.

Halberd and Usuthu looked down at him, first with annoyance, then with slowly increasing mirth.

"Mälar," said Halberd, "can you not respect this moment? At last we communicate with the natives of this land. Must you mock him?"

"I am sorry," Mälar sputtered, "but to fear these men, to flee them and to kill them, and then to finally hear the name of our valiant enemy. And what a name! Oh, they'll sing of our glory to our memory around the fires in winter. Hah! All hail the conquerors of Two Dogs!"

He laughed again.

Labrans sat with no expression. Two Dogs watched Mälar with care.

"His laughter does not seem to insult the Skræling," Usuthu said. "Indeed, it reduces his fear."

Two Dogs did look a bit more calm. Despite the vomit soaking into his clothes and drying on his chin, he still maintained the regal dignity characteristic of the Skrælings.

"Mälar," said Halberd, "since you find this warrior so amusing, bring some water and clean him. Give him a drink."

Mälar carried water from the spring in a skin. He splashed some onto the ropes that held the Skræling to Labrans and poured more over his soiled leggings. Two Dogs watched him warily, as if kindness from an enemy signaled forthcoming treachery.

When Mälar offered him a drink, Two Dogs snapped his jaws shut. Mälar drank, to show the purity of the water, then profferred the skin again. Two Dogs looked away.

"Ask him," said Halberd, "who he believes we are."

Two Dogs spoke at some length.

"We are the white-skinned demons who are made of fur," Labrans said woodenly. "We have come to kill their children and enslave their women. This," Labrans indicated Usuthu with a pointing chin, "is the black white man who is not made of fur, but of two suns."

"Black white man?" said Usuthu.

"What does he mean," Halberd said, " 'made of fur'?"

Labrans listened with care, and again spoke like a man without a soul.

"They wear skins, not furs. They have never seen fur used as a garment. They think it is part of your skin. Further, they have never seen hair grow upon a man's face. They believe it also is fur. Never have they seen hair color like yours, except in the pelts of the fox and the bear.

"They believe, therefore, that you are half-man and half-animal. Usuthu they take for an evil god. They have no metal. They believe his shields are two suns stolen from the sky and worn for protection."

Halberd looked at Usuthu in amazement. Usuthu's face bore no expression. Halberd knew that Usuthu was carefully documenting the language of the Skrælings. Usuthu's wide roamings with the armies of the Great Khan had taught him many tongues. He had an ear for strange languages. The little he heard now, he would remember.

Usuthu leaned forward. The strong bones of his black face gleamed in the golden glow.

"Where," hissed Usuthu, "lies his army?"

Labrans spoke, then listened, then spoke again: "They make their way down the cliffs above the falls. During the night they shall climb. They did not expect us here for some weeks."

"And the witch?" Halberd spoke in the faintest of whispers, though he believed his voice echoed in the cave.

"She leads the men, alternately appearing and disappearing. She never walks, but travels by spell. A fearsome half-man walks beside her at all times."

"Surely," said Halberd, "that is the Dwarf, Suttung, slayer of my brother. He replaces Thund as her bodyguard and evil servant."

"There is more," said Labrans. "She comes to the men at night, and is their lover. There are more than thirty men in her band and every night she is lover to all of them, one at a time yet all at once. She lies in their tents with all of them during the night though they sleep many feet apart, and most in their own dwellings. It does not matter. She is alone with every man, yet she is with every man. She is everywhere at once."

Two Dogs spoke again, unbidden, in an unmistakable tone, no matter what the language.

"She is," translated Labrans, "a bewitching lover, the best Two Dogs has ever enjoyed. If Two Dogs sleeps beside another man and Two Dogs makes love to Grettir, he cannot see Grettir with the other man, yet that man swears he, too, is Grettir's lover."

"Halberd, my boy," said Mälar, "her magic is ferocious. Can we resist her?"

Halberd turned from the bound warrior and his brother. He stepped over the log wall and rested his forehead on the cool, slick rock. His heart pounded. His head throbbed. He beat one fist softly on the rock.

There was no mistaking it: The rage that coursed through him was jealousy. He hated the Skrælings for being the lovers of Grettir! How dare she enslave them with love? How dare she use the same passion that tore at Halberd to rule a few pitiful savages?

Whence came these unwanted feelings? How could he still bear such lust for the witch? How deep into his souls did her claws reach? How could any man call himself a true warrior and yet have no control over the urges of his heart?

Halberd looked to the eternal falls, into the green curtain that glowed ghostly silver from the moonlight. Below him, the Skrælings doubtless massed at the base of the cliff, driven by their natural love of battle and their unnatural lust for Grettir.

Driven as he was driven.

How could he escape her clutches?

"The answer," her voice rang through the cave, "is that you cannot!"

Halberd turned in horror, automatically reaching for his broadsword. It lay across the room with his armor.

Halberd vaulted the log wall. Labrans still sat on the floor, his face twitching and his eyes bulging. The golden glow around him whipped and snarled, lifting away from him and settling back down. The jewel and the knife began to turn over and over him, faster and faster. Mälar leapt to his feet and made for the ax. Usuthu raised his silver mallet and opened his mouth to cast a spell.

The golden glow surrounding Labrans turned jet black.

It closed around him like a fist. The jewel and Hrungnir spun in the air like a wheel, like a top, like a dancing dervish from the Land of Sand. They spun too fast to be seen. Labrans seemed to swell. His muscles seemed to grow. The rope binding him bulged outward.

The black band exploded.

Mälar was thrown across the cave. Usuthu flew backward into the log wall. An avalanche of logs buried him. Halberd was knocked flat. The knife shot across the room in one direction and the jewel in another. The point of the knife hit the rock wall. The knife sank into the wall to its hilt.

Labrans stood, the rope in tatters around his feet. His eyes glowed and his chest heaved. The black glow surrounded him with fiendish energy. Labrans looked behind him and yanked Two Dogs to his feet.

Stunned, Halberd lay on his back and fought to draw a breath.

"How I have longed for this moment!" Labrans threw back his head and yowled like a she-wolf. He raised his open palms to the sky. A mad grin split his face.

"And you, you big-mouthed coward," Labrans screamed, "you die first!"

Labrans snatched Two Dogs off the ground. Halberd struggled to his feet as Labrans, carrying the kicking and swinging Skræling in two hands, effortlessly vaulted the wall and raced for the cave entrance.

Halberd knew Labrans desired Hrungnir above all else. He staggered across the cave towards the knife. Usuthu tossed a thick log off his chest and tried to stand. Labrans slid to a sudden stop at the very edge of the cave. He slung Two Dogs behind him, holding him parallel to the cave floor with both hands, gaining momentum for a fiendish throw. Labrans bent at the knees and whipped his hands forward. He flung Two Dogs with demonic strength.

Two Dogs sailed into the night. It was impossible. Two Dogs did not fall. He kept going and going. His braids trailed behind him. His arms clutched outward but grabbed only air.

Through the uprising mist, through the cloudless, moonlit night, Two Dogs soared over the churning rapids, not falling, but rising, sailing even higher, only to crash into the endlessly replenished green wall of the Thundering Falls.

Strong as Labrans was, he lacked the strength to fling Two Dogs through that moving wall of water. The falls smashed Two Dogs into its remorseless current and out of sight.

Labrans spun around the face of the cave. His fists clenched and unclenched. He smiled with all his teeth. His eyes glowed like a rabid wolf's. Halberd saw none of it. He braced one weak foot on the wall and worked at Hrungnir with his strengthless hands. The knife would not come free.

Again Labrans hopped the log wall, making straight for Halberd. As he cleared the wall, Usuthu flung a square-ended log against his legs from behind. Labrans tangled with the log and fell face-first to the cave floor.

Mälar gained his feet across the cave and called a warning to Halberd.

Labrans moved more quickly than a panther. At the sound of Mälar's voice, Labrans scooped up the log between his legs and whipped it across the length of the cave. It took Mälar full in the chest and hurled him into a heap in the mud.

The black glow surrounding Labrans crackled with energy. Labrans scooped up Halberd's great ax and raced toward his brother. Understanding the demon's quickness, knowing he had no time, Usuthu tore the silver mallet off his neck and flicked it end over end at the demon.

Halberd saw none of it. He yanked at Hrungnir with all his might. The smell of burning filled the cave, no doubt from the black glow.

Though scurrying at unbelievable speed toward Halberd, Labrans spun and held the flat of the ax toward the flying mallet. The magical hammer struck the ax and bent it with a horrible clang! but Labrans was not staggered. The mallet bounced off and rang against the rock floor.

As the Mongol reached his feet and took his bow in his hands, he bellowed to Halberd. He knew he was too late.

Labrans was already upon his brother. Labrans drew back the ax and launched a killing blow at Halberd's back.

As the bent blade whistled down, some final vestige of family love and loyalty fought the witch's spell in Labrans' heart. With the blade inches from its target and moving like lightning, Labrans betrayed his mistress. The words leapt from his mouth unbidden.

"Halberd," Labrans screamed with all his heart, "beware your brother!"

Halberd flinched to one side. The ax did not split his spine. Instead it buried to the handle into his left shoulder and upper back. He fell onto the cave floor without a sound. His blood pumped out around the blade.

Labrans stared at his brother, trying to understand what he had done. In that moment of human weakness, the witch reasserted her control. Labrans smiled his horrible smile and reached overhead for the haft of Hrungnir.

Usuthu's arrow cleanly pierced Labrans' hand. The iron point yanked his hand into the wall and then clanged off, shattering the arrowhead and filling Labrans' hand with fragments. Labrans turned to face Usuthu and another arrow split his thigh. The head burst through the back of his leg and hurled him to the floor. Usuthu flung down his bow, drew his bronze sword, and charged.

Mälar stood at the end of the cave. He hunched over, feeling his chest for broken ribs. Spitting blood, the old man drew his stabbing knife and shuffled toward Labrans.

Labrans pulled himself to his feet. He raised one hand toward the Mongol. Labrans' arm was lifted until it was even with his shoulder. His finger aimed square at the Mongol's heart.

The black glow sparked off Labrans' fingers. Usuthu felt himself lifted from the cave floor and hurled toward the cave mouth. He flew backward, his legs in front of him and his useless sword in his hand. He saved himself only by plunging the sword down into the log wall. The blade caught as Usuthu fell into the tumbled logs.

Labrans flashed past the Mongol and swung out the cave mouth. He vanished down the slick rock wall, climbing as cleanly as a spider.

Usuthu looked across the cave. Halberd lay unconscious, his life pumping out into the dark brown mud.

Under the Thundering Falls

Usuthu knelt over Halberd. He pulled gently at the ax. It was deeply embeded in Halberd's flesh.

"To yank it free" he called to Mälar, "might cause even more bleeding."

"Have you herbs for such a wound?"

"No," the Mongol answered. "I would gather my healing plants fresh from the ground, if I could reach it."

"What of your magic mallet?" Mälar asked. "Can you seal the wound with its power?"

Usuthu shook his head bitterly.

"The mallet is a vehicle for dealing with Immortals," he said. "I never should have thrown it at Labrans. I may have weakened its power or even broken the bond that has bound that hammer to my family for forty generations. No one in history has used it against a mortal, even though that mortal is demonic.

"You saw, it functioned only as a thrown hammer. It had no power to contest Labrans. I cannot use it to save Halberd. It would not work, and I would destroy a spiritual bond older than time."

"So be it, Usuthu," Mälar said gently. "If you cannot, you cannot. We must save him as we would any man on the battlefield."

Mälar pulled off his ragged tunic and cut it into strips. Usuthu went to the rear of the cave and emptied his bladder into the mud. The mud made by his voiding he gathered into this hands and carried back to Mälar.

"I see no spiderwebs in this cold cave," Usuthu said, "so we must use the oldest poultice known to man."

"Despite its age," Mälar said, "it works. Dump your piss-mud beside me and help me remove the ax."

Mälar held the edges of Halberd's fearsome wound together while Usuthu gently worked the axblade. He tugged gently upward and then pulled downward, as softly as he could. With each movement, new spurts of blood pulsed out beside the blade. The bent ax came out slowly. When only the edge of the blade remained in Halberd's flesh, the flow of blood was great.

"Cut him out of his tunic," Mälar said. "Do not pull the ax all the way free. Cut his garment into strips."

Usuthu worked his slashing knife with hands too fast to see. Halberd's shirt hung off him in long, even stripes.

Mälar gathered a small handful of the piss-mud and worked it carefully around the edge of the axblade. The bloodflow slowed. Mälar watched carefully, not daring to jar the blade. As the flood lessened, Mälar shifted the blade slightly, packing more mud in around its sharp edge.

Usuthu watched impatiently, working his hands up and down the haft of his curved bronze sword.

"Do not fear," Mälar said, "I believe we may save him."

"He will live," the Mongol said without inflection. "I know how to ensure that he will. What concerns me is that Labrans might also live."

Mälar said nothing. He swabbed the wound carefully with a strip of cloth.

"When you no longer need my help here, old man," Usuthu whispered, his mouth full of hate, "I shall track that traitor and chop him into pieces."

"Do not despair so," said Mälar. "Halberd wished his brother kept alive. He knew this might occur. He ran this risk like a man."

"Yes, he faced the risk bravely. He followed his heart. He could not slay his brother. Therefore, it was our task to protect him. We failed. I failed. If I cannot kill Labrans then I am not a man, not a true warrior and certainly not the blood-brother of Halberd."

"Hold that cloth to the wound. I will pull the ax free."

Mälar moved the ax the final half inch from Halberd's ripped flesh. The puckered skin clung to the blade. Mälar washed the blade with wet cloth and gradually peeled Halberd from the blade. The edges of the wound were dead white. Halberd's ribs shone. All were broken by the ax, as was his collarbone and the wide bone in his upper back. Mälar peered closely inside his friend.

Without looking at Usuthu, Mälar spoke quietly, "What of the Skræling horde climbing the cliff at this moment."

"I will kill as many of those I can while I climb down. The remainder are your problem."

The piss-mud had staunched the internal bleeding. The cavity of the wound was not refilling with blood. Mälar steered the broken ends of the ribs together as best as he could. He did likewise to the collarbone.As he ground the shattered bones against one another, Halberd moaned and jerked, but he did not awaken.

"Thank you," said Mälar, "for your show of confidence in my abilities. But if you do not fear thirty Skrælings, what of one witch?"

"We need not concern ourselves with her for a while," Usuthu answered. "With each great show of strength she is weakened. To break Halberd's spell was exhausting work. She will leave our death to her warriors.

"After all, she doubtless believes Halberd to be dead. She has no reason to think we can survive the upcoming attack. She will not show herself until the assault is done."

Mälar nodded to Usuthu. The Mongol raised Halberd's chest and slid a long cloth under him. Mälar pulled his fingers out of the wound. He daubed away the last bit of dirt and piss-mud. He then washed out the wound with a weak stream of water from a skin. Usuthu passed the cloth strip around Halberd and formed a knot. Mälar nodded again.

Usuthu drew the knot tight, then tighter still. Halberd moaned with pain that shot through him despite his unconsciousness. Working swiftly, Mälar and Halberd drew several strips around Halberd. When they stopped, Halberd's chest was wrapped as tightly as a dead, preserved king in the Land of Sand on the Inland Sea.

Mälar sat back on his haunches and drew a long drink from the skin.

"If you are right about the witch," he said, "then we may survive the Skrælings. If you are wrong, we will not. In any case, what of our brother?"

"Check the cliff, old man," Usuthu said. "I will do what I must for Halberd. If the Skrælings are near enough to deter by rolling a few logs on them, do so by all means."

Mälar climbed over what remained of the log wall. Mälar had not confessed it, but he loathed heights. He did not want to approach the cliff. He lay on his stomach and slid forward. He hung his head over the cliff.

The blood and magic of Labrans' escape had driven the beauty of the Thundering Falls right out of his head. The noise was so constant it was easy to forget. As Mälar looked out over the boiling pool, the majesty of the place filled his heart with hope, and pride in the spirit of the Northmen.

The green water slid endlessly down in the glowing moonlight. The waters churned and spun, throwing plumes of mist halfway up the cliff. It was a peaceful scene.

Mälar gazed directly below him. His breath caught in his throat. The cliff was swarming with Skrælings. They climbed easily and without fear. All were doubtless enchanted. They wore bows and lances, bashing mallets and sharp-edged hatchets. There were a lot of them.

Feathers glistened in their hair and animal-claw necklaces clicked against their bare chests. Paint was slashed on their faces and ran down their arms and backs.

Mälar crawled on his belly back to the log wall. He chose one log with care and rolled it in front of him. He rolled it to the cliff edge and gently shoved it over the side.

The log fell straight down, hugging the cliff wall as it tumbled. It turned upright in midair and took one warrior in the top of his head with a loud chunk! He dropped off the cliff and into the chest of his brother below him. The two fell into the rapids without a sound. None of their brothers turned to watch them go.

"Aye, Usuthu," Mälar cried with excitement, "that was fun. I might slay half of them with logs as weapons . . . what are you doing?"

Usuthu rooted like a dog at the base of the large woodpile. Hrungnir he clasped tightly in one hand. A large hole gleamed on the cliff-wall where Hrungnir had been imbedded.

"I'm looking," Usuthu replied without stopping,

"for the jewel. It landed somewhere under these logs."

"How did you free the knife? Halberd could not budge it."

"I bashed the cave wall with my silver mallet."

"Usuthu," Mälar said with great patience, "you told me the mallet was to be used only against Immortals."

"I lost my temper, old man!" Usuthu roared. "Now, shut up and help me search for the jewel."

"Uhm, Usuthu, perhaps you do not realize . . . I cannot. The Skrælings are halfway to our door and logs are proving most effective against them."

"Suit yourself," the Mongol growled. He dismissed Mälar with a wave of his hand. Logs flew over his shoulder as he rooted after the jewel.

Mälar returned to the ledge. Feeling a bit bolder now, he held a small log upright and released it. It plucked another Eerhahkwoi from the cliff. His head exploded like a melon when the log struck him. He fell away from the cliff in a jumble of cartwheeling arms and legs. Unfortunately, he took no one else with him. It was too dark to see the insignificant splash he made when he hit.

"Mälar," called Usuthu, "come quickly. I've found it."

Usuthu stood over Halberd, who had not moved. His back rose and fell at irregular intervals, weakly. Blood spotted his bandages. Halberd held the jewel in one hand and Hrungnir in the other.

"Will you heal him with the knife?"

"No," Usuthu answered. "The knife is his to command. It will not answer me. I hope instead to combine it with the jewel and cast Halberd's spirit into the Dream World. His lover there should know how to care for him."

"What would you have me do?"

"Watch me to ensure that I do as he did."

"Usuthu, I will not," Mälar answered. "You are a holy man. I am not. I cannot pray and will not make magic. I never have.

"You are shaken by the nearness of our brother's death and so you wish my company even though you do not need my counsel. I shall not give you either.

"We are attacked. I must defend us. Further, you must find your own strength at this moment. I cannot give you mine. I need it. Look into your heart and you will cast the spell correctly. Indeed, how could you not? You are, after all, Halberd's brother in spirit and in blood. Do what you must to save him and us. I shall do the same.

"Now, leave me alone."

Mälar returned to the cave mouth, where he chose and dropped his logs with great care. Usuthu shook his head. He had not been lashed like that since his childhood. He knelt over Halberd and whispered into his ear. "My brother, your body is without awareness but the spirit never sleeps. Guide my hand with these tools and fly to your Dream World. Do not return until you are healed, however long that may take. Mälar and I will protect you, if I don't first throw Mälar into the falls for his insolent mouth.

"As you sleep, know that Labrans is slain. I vow to kill him. Whether that brings you joy or sorrow I cannot know. Nor do I care.

"Now, guide me."

Usuthu stood over Halberd and pressed the two objects toward each another. They resisted him and would not draw near enough to start the spell.

Usuthu pushed again.

"I am Usuthu of the Great Steppes," he called. "Warrior, holy man and son of warriors of the Great Khans for centuries. I call upon your magic on behalf of my brother, Halberd, Dream Warrior. Cast your healing spell over him and bear him where he cannot ask to be carried. Bear him to the Dream World and into the arms of his lover.

"Protect him from the witch on his journey."

Usuthu clasped the two together with all his might.

"I," he grunted for a breath, "beseech you ..." and another ... "save my brother ..." one last gasp and mighty shove ... "Now!"

The jewel left his hand. Hrungnir floated softly up after it. They moved away from Usuthu, borne on invisible currents, and hovered over Halberd. There they floated smoothly toward one another and locked together, the jewel fitting tightly inside Hrungnir for the first time.

Their glow was not golden, but a brighter, silvery, sunlike aura. Usuthu averted his eyes. The glow settled over Halberd like a blanket. He shone as brightly as a sun. He bled no more. His breath came more readily, as if his pain had stopped. He seemed at peace.

Usuthu let out a long pent-up breath. He carried the blood- and flesh-coated ax to Mälar and laid it by his feet. The old man stood on the edge of the cliff, his toes over the precipice, oblivious to the height. He dropped one small log with the precision of a smith forging a magic blade. Seconds later, three splashes sounded; one for the log, one each for the two Skrælings.

Mälar turned back to the Mongol.

"Well?" he snapped.

Usuthu strapped on his curved sword and his dagger. The mallet hung from his neck.

"Halberd sleeps peacefully. I believe he has found the Dream World. Do not move him, do not disturb him. If he can be healed, he will be healed there."

"What of your bow?"

"I want to kill Labrans with my hands. I will not bring it."

"If you do carry it," Mälar said, "you might slay a few of the Skrælings once you reach the ground. They may still be on the cliff."

"Very well," Usuthu answered, "but once below I do not wish to tarry. Labrans flees as we speak."

"Kill but a few, to ease my way," Mälar said. "Already I have killed seven. There are only a few more than twenty remaining. Reduce their number and I'll have a better chance."

"How will you fight them?"

"I am but a poor archer, but soon they will be near enough to provide even me with a reliable target. I'll use Halberd's bow on those I may hit and his ax on those I may not. My stabbing knife will I use on those I cannot chop."

"Farewell, old man," Usuthu said, extending his arm. "I'll not return until I've struck Labrans' head from his shoulders, however long that may take."

Mälar took his forearm in the grip of comradeship.

"Kill him, Usuthu, then return here and help me kill the Eerhahkwoi. But on your return slay a deer or an elk. We have but little remaining."

"That I shall. Thank you for your sound advice moments before. You said you would not give me your strength, but you did."

"Did I?" the navigator replied. "Possibly. Now go. May Bahaad Dahaabs protect you."

Usuthu smiled in surprise.

"And you, old man."

He made his way to the cliff, swung one leg over the edge, and was gone.

Mälar nocked an arrow into his bow and peered over the cliff.

Halberd walks along the path in the woods. He feels no pain. His body is light and alive. He stands on the crest of the hill, where he last gazed down with deep bitterness. As he watches, the flap of Ishlanawanda's tent flings open. At this distance she is a slender silhouette. She looks up the hillside, waves to Halberd and runs out of her village to the trail.

Halberd trots down the trail toward her. He winds through the forest, his breath coming in gasps, the familiar sense of peace and contentment enveloping him like a cloak. He moves through the tall redwood trees, through the patches of sunlight. He sees her at a bend in the trail.

She races toward him, running on her toes, her hair flying behind her. Halberd stands, waiting for her to draw near.

She leaps the final few steps and springs into his arms. She is alive and strong, as real as anyone in the Waking World. He feels her tremble. He feels her supple strength and the muscles in her sides, stomach and back. He feels her nipples rise under her long deerskin dress.

Neither speaks. Ishlanawanda rests her head on his chest, sobbing quietly.

"Why . . ." Halberd pauses to gain control of his emotions. One more spoken word would send tears down his cheeks.

"Why," he tries again, "are you able to touch me?"

Ishlanawanda looks up at him with surprise.

"Do you," she asked, "bear Hrungnir?"

Halberd reaches down for his armor. For some reason he is not wearing it. He feels a stab of fear.

"My love," he says, "I have left without my weapons. I must return."

"Hold," she whispers urgently. "Make no move to leave. Examine yourself."

Halberd looks at his arms. They glow white-hot, bursting with magic. So too, are his legs, his chest, his hair.

"Is this my protection?"

"Know you not," Ishlanawanda asks, "the circumstances of your coming here?"

"No. I cannot recall."

"The witch assaulted you via the instrument of your poor brother. He may have slain you with your own ax. I do not yet know if your body in the Waking World will survive."

Halberd sits down on a stump, holding tightly to Ishlanawanda's hand.

"Will I die here if my body dies?"

"Yes, but I have much magic here with which to heal you. Together we shall keep your spirit strong. If your body survives, you will survive."

"Is there jeopardy beyond my wound?"

"Eerhahkwoi under the spell of Grettir attack your cave."

Halberd jumps to his feet distractedly, searching for a weapon.

"I must return and aid Mälar and Usuthu!"

"Halberd," Ishlanawanda speaks gently, "you may do nothing. If you return to your body in the Waking World you will die. If you remain here I shall keep your spirit strong and you may live. If Mälar does not defeat the Eerhahkwoi then they will doubtless bear your hapless body to Grettir.

"Here you are safe from her. You carry Hrungnir's protection even though you do not carry Hrungnir. My elders welcome you to the village. If you conduct yourself as a warrior you will be accepted and allowed to stay."

"What of my comrades, who fight without me?"

"Despair, self-hatred and guilt are killers of the

spirit. Feel none of them," Ishlanawanda speaks sweetly into his ear. "Usuthu cast you here to survive. Enjoy our time together and let me heal you from within."

She leads Halberd down the trail to her village.

Usuthu worked his way down the slick black rock. The Skrælings were just below. If they were concentrating as he did, they would not look up. They would not see him. Mälar rolled no more logs down the cliff. He would wait until Usuthu was on the rocks below, and then he would protect himself with his bow.

Usuthu had to climb quickly. The longer he took, the more time the Skrælings had to near the cave. He looked between his feet. Between him and the pounding rapids below came four Skrælings climbing more or less in a line and climbing on Usuthu's route down.

The Mongol froze on the cliff. He slid his sword out of his scabbard and ducked his head into the rock wall. The lead Eerhahkwoi reached Usuthu's feet. He stretched one hand up and seized Usuthu's lower leg. Usuthu dug in with his hands and swung his leg out from the cliff.

The shocked Skræling clutched instinctively for the moving leg and found himself dangling over the abyss. Bracing on one hand and one foot, Usuthu swung his sword in a brief, chopping arc and severed the hands of the Eerhahkwoi from his arms. The Skræling fell straight back into two below him. They vanished into the mist, grunting in surprise.

Usuthu pried the tip of his sword into the hands that still clutched his leg and flipped them into the roaring rapids. Those Skrælings below him moved sideways. They seemed intent on gaining the cave. They did not wish to fight on the cliff.

Usuthu moved down as rapidly as he dared. He could not bear to climb the last twenty feet and so dropped from the cliff to the jagged rocks below. He hit gracefully but his feet went out from under him on the wet rock. He toppled forward and embraced the rock with all his heart. The water churned by inches from his face. It sought to tear him from the rock.

His jaw banged shut and his teeth trapped his tongue, but he held on. After a moment he regained his footing. He stood and backed from the cliff until he stood just inside the curtain of water. Usuthu raised his bow.

He had but seven arrows remaining. Usuthu drew on the Skræling nearest the top, but before he could fire, his target fell off the cliff and tumbled down, an arrow sticking through his chest. The Skræling bounced off the cliff on his way down.

Usuthu chose his next target and fired. The angle was difficult; Usuthu was shooting almost straight over his head. His arrow threw sparks off the cliff before it penetrated the Skræling's back. His head dropped onto his chest and he slid down the cliff, never raising his arms or moving his legs.

Usuthu shot another and hunkered down on the jagged rocks. This warrior flew straight at Usuthu's head. He landed on the rocks above Usuthu, spraying him with blood and flesh.

Usuthu rapidly emptied his quiver. Every shot found its target. Fewer than twenty now climbed. Usuthu calculated that Mälar could kill at least five more before they would gain the cave. He should be able to shoot another five from the log wall. That would leave less than ten for hand-to-hand. The odds were favorable.

Usuthu slung his bow and rested it on the jagged pile of rocks. He stepped around the edge of the Thundering Falls and raced along the path that followed the top of the gorge.

Halberd rests with his back against a log by the gentle river some distance from the village. Ishlanawanda and he sit in a shaded glade, eating quietly, watching the river flow. She sits beside him, caressing his forehead and smiling into his eyes.

"How I have longed for you," she says. "My elders bade me to take a husband, but none had my gifts. No one knew what I know. I waited. I have been waiting. I knew when I saw you that you would be my lover. Since then, I have waited for you."

"Are you aware of my lust for Grettir? Do you know that we were lovers?"

"Once," Ishlanawanda says playful. "You were lovers but one time. As for the lust in your heart, it is not as strong as you think. It is the only spell Grettir has over you. I shall break it."

Ishlanawanda leans over Halberd. She kisses his

neck, then slowly works her mouth down over his shoulders, his upper arm, his back. Her full lips slide over his muscular flesh. Her clean black hair wafts over his face and chest.

"I shall kiss you," she whispers, "every place that Labrans harmed you with your ax. My kisses will heal you."

"I believe," replies Halberd, feeling lust in his loins to equal the love in his heart, "that they shall."

"Oh," Ishlanawanda whispered, sliding to sit in his lap, "they shall, they shall."

She buries her head into his shoulder, licking him with her hot, wet tongue. Her smooth, firm thighs curl around his waist and hold him tightly.

"And yours," she breaths into his ear, "shall heal me."

Mälar watched Usuthu drop his bow and vanish around the corner of the Thundering Falls. Mälar could no longer hear it. His heart pounded too loudly. He felt no fear. Only elation. His sweat-slick hands opened and closed on the Skræling bow.

A quick count over the edge told him fourteen Skrælings still climbed. He looked down at them, filled with lust for their blood. He drew carefully down on the shoulders of his nearest target. They were too near to aim for any other spot.

The first one lost his grip when the arrow slammed into him. He hung on with his other hand. Mälar wasted one of his dwindling arrows by shooting him in the opposite shoulder. The Skræling grabbed for handholds and footholds all the way down. He was harder to kill than the others. He died anyway.

The next Eerhahkwoi looked right into Mälar's eyes as the Northmen released.

"Die, Skræling!" the navigator screamed.

The Skræling screamed back in a voice full of defiance. The arrow went into his mouth and exploded the back of his head. The shattered head drooped, but the hands did not let go of the slick rocks. The dead warrior hung as his brothers scrambled past him.

Mälar felt no remorse, only joy. At last, after weeks of running and hiding and fighting with magic, at last, here was battle, man-to-man, hand-to-hand, for no glory, for no territory, but, as the Gods intended man to fight, for pure life itself.

"Come and kill me," he screamed at the Skrælings, beside himself with rapture. "Kill me and send my poor aging backside to Aasgard. If you can."

Mälar picked another off the cliff.

"If you can!"

The remaining twelve were too near to shoot. Mälar flipped a log off the edge without looking to see what damage it did. He crouched next to the edge, Halberd's ax raised over his shoulder, breathing easily and ready to strike.

Usuthu had found Labrans' trail. He ran through briars. He ran through brambles. He ran through places a rabbit couldn't go. Usuthu ran so fast that

Gevrm, the Hound of Hell, could not catch him. He ran all the way along the top of the gorge.

Labrans fled, but he was no longer enchanted. His trail was too well marked, too rushed, too lacking in strategy. Without the aid of Grettir, Labrans was not an exceptional warrior. In fact, thought Usuthu, he was not exceptional in any way. Labrans had not lost the new strength that enchantment had granted him. He covered much more ground than Usuthu had thought he would. No one could match Usuthu's stride, and he made one step for every three of Labrans'.

Usuthu raced along the twisting path, diverging from it and sprinting through the rough woods where Labrans' trail diverged, returning to it when the Northman had apparently enough of being scratched by thorns and stung by nettles.

The river tore down the narrow gorge below the narrow, winding path, flinging white water onto the trail itself, obscuring Labrans' footprints. It did not matter. Usuthu could smell him, could feel him, could think the thoughts in his mind.

Usuthu's blood beat in the hearts of the finest hunters in the world. He could track a hare over twenty leagues of solid stone. One swift Viking was no chore. Usuthu tumbled into a dense thicket. The tracks through the grass were deep. The thicket ended in a small clearing. Thick thorny trees and choking underbrush sealed the clearing on all four sides.

Waiting on the other side of the clearing was Labrans. Very little moonlight penetrated, but

Usuthu could see the gleam of Labrans' teeth as he smiled his wolflike smile.

Labrans hefted the sword he had stolen from Mälar. It glinted briefly in the moonlight, and then was lowered. Usuthu slid his curved bronze sword from his scabbard.

His heart singing, Usuthu stepped forward.

Ishlanawanda fills Halberd's mouth with her eager tongue. Her kisses are those of a young woman filled with passion, which she is. But they are also the wild kisses of an inexperienced young girl, which she also is. She runs her light, deft hands up and down Halberd's chest, moaning as he takes her sweet breasts into his hands.

Halberd wraps his hands in her luxurious black hair and holds her tightly. He turns her face up to him. She stares back with her rich brown eyes, ready to do his bidding. Her lips part. Halberd crushes her mouth with his own. His hands slide under her long deerskin dress, along her warm thighs and cup her young, muscular rump. She writhes on his lap, gently pulling her hair back and forth across his face.

His fingers slip inside her. She grabs his shoulders and turns her face to the clear blue sky, gasping with pleasure. She bucks back and forth on his rapidly moving fingers, moaning his name in a hoarse whisper.

She shakes herself gently on his fingers, then plunges down hard upon them, then raises herself almost off them once more. Her eyes glaze. Sweet drops of perspiration break out along her upper lip.

"Oh, Halberd," she breathes into his open mouth, "I can wait no longer."

With one last wriggle she pulls herself off his questing hands. Halberd cannot draw a breath. His desire for Grettir is nothing to what now courses through him. His love for Ishlanawanda fills his heart. Her exquisite face, made so much more beautiful by the unchecked desire she feels, drives him to be inside her.

She raises herself off his lap and extends a hand to pull him to his feet. She fumbles with the ties on his leggings and yanks them down his legs. She takes him into her gentle hands and looks into his eyes. He reaches out to pull off her deerskin dress.

"No, my love," she speaks in a voice almost too hoarse to hear, "I cannot wait even for that."

She turns her back to him and gracefully bends over the log. Halberd steps forward and pushes her dress well up her back. Her brown body is lean and firm. When she stretches forward all the muscles under her skin stand defined. She reaches back for him and guides him into her. She flinches and then nods as he enters her. As he moves inside her, she nods again and again, smiling with all her heart.

"This," she moans, "is what I imagined."

She is soft and hot and wet. Halberd eases himself into her. Ishlanawanda shakes her long black hair and gasps with each of Halberd's movements. Her body twitches back against him. Her mouth speaks words that none but she and Halberd may understand.

When Halberd is fully inside her, he gently pulls back and drives forward, rocking her on the log and on the hands that reach out in front of her for support. Once, twice, he moves into her as slowly as he can stand.

Gasping and softly grunting, Ishlanawanda makes a short pumping motion with her hips. She pushes back at him. She urges him to drive into her deeper, faster, longer. Her clenched fists make rapid, thrusting gestures.

Unaware of his surroundings, his name, or even which world he is in, Halberd plunges into the lovely Skræling woman who loves him, his Dream Lover, plunges in and pulls out, plunges in and pulls out, his heart bursting with love, while she drives back at him, her long thighs holding him smoothly, her head bucking and shaking, her sweet voice calling his name over and over between her gasps of pleasure.

Mälar did not hesitate when the first hand gripped the edge of the cliff. He chopped all the fingers off it and listened with satisfaction as the Skræling bounced down the cliff.

Four more hands seized the ledge. Mälar chopped two of them off and bent his knees as an Eerhahkwoi head popped up. This Eerhahkwoi was quick. He raised his hatchet with his other hand and made a menacing gesture at Mälar.

"Am I supposed," the old man asked as he stepped

forward and sent the Skræling's head soaring out over the rapids, "to be fearful of you while one hand holds the ledge? Are you so stupid?"

Blood gushed from the headless neck and soaked the cliff edge. When Mälar raised one foot to kick the body off the cliff his foot slipped and he went sprawling into the blood.

Two more Eerhahkwoi hopped onto the ledge. One raised a bashing mallet with a huge stone head and the other a stone-headed lance. On his back, Mälar chopped one Skræling's foot in half, lengthwise. As he did, the mallet swung down. Mälar snatched his head back. The stone head whistled by. He yanked his stabbing knife from his belt and plunged it into the belly of the Eerhahkwoi who had dared to swing at him.

That warrior folded at the waist and dropped to his knees. The other sat down hard and stared at his devastated foot in puzzlement. Mälar scrambled to his feet, slipping and sliding. He snatched his ax out of the Skræling's foot. He backpedaled as several more warriors gained the ledge.

Mälar faked as if he would jump over the log wall. When two of the warriors stepped forward to pursue him, Mälar leaned into them. One swung backhanded with a short lance and slashed Mälar across the face. Mälar buried the ax in his chest. The other Mälar stabbed deep in the side. He fell over in that direction.

The Skræling who bore the ax fell straight back but unfortunately, not over the cliff edge. Three more gained the ledge as he fell towards them. Six Skrælings now faced Mälar.

Mälar jumped the log wall and hurled the largest log he could lift right into their midst. It took one in the crotch and cast him over the edge, his legs straight up in the air. Mälar raised Halberd's broadsword and gestured them forward.

"Let's fight!" he murmured. "Let's see how a Northman dies!"

One Eerhahkwoi took a thoughtful step backward. Two more came forward. Mälar kicked the top section of the wall at them and stepped in behind the rolling logs. One wide swing slashed a Skræling neck like a chicken and smashed the arm from the body of another. Blood jetted out of the severed neck in a horizontal stream.

"This is quite a sword," the navigator screamed. "Its balance is without peer."

Mälar wrenched his sword free and took a crushing blow on his left arm. The arm went dead. Mälar could not feel his blood trickling down it. He shifted to a one-hand grip on Halberd's massive sword and stood a step back.

Mälar shook his head to throw his dripping blood out of his eyes. He knew he dared not retreat. Bloodlust and fear kept him invincible. If he thought for one instant he was doomed. . . .

Two advanced. One still hung back. Mälar turned sideways to them and drew the sword parallel to his shoulder in a maneuver he had learned from the yellow-skinned merchants who visited the Land of Sand. They were great, nimble swordsmen.

When Mälar raised the sword, its blade caught glints of the golden light surrounding Halberd's body. The two warriors stared up at the slowly revolving knife and jewel. They were momentarily transfixed.

"Know not where you are, you fools?" Mälar roared. "Fight with all your skills! Bah! Do not disappoint me."

He jumped at them and plunged Halberd's sword into one Skræling's heart. The blade stuck fast, held by ribs. Mälar left it behind. With his good hand he punched the other Skræling in the neck. The warrior sank to his knees, choking. His face turned purple under his brown skin.

"You," Mälar said to the choking Eerhahkwoi, "are a dead man. No more air will reach your lungs. You will die in a few minutes. Enjoy it."

Mälar stood erect. The blood ran down his face. He licked his lips. It tasted good. His left arm hung at his side, useless. The Skræling he punched in the throat seemed to have cut him with a hatchet. Mälar's right shoulder bled freely.

"What are you waiting for?" Mälar screamed at the last of the Eerhahkwoi. "Let's die together, as men of war should die."

The Eerhahkwoi observed Mälar with care. He lay down his lance. He hefted a blood-stained hatchet in his right hand and a stone-headed mallet in his left. He took one cautious step. His knees were bent. His head was up.

Mälar smiled with glee. He had no weapons. He had but one arm. He could barely see.

"Do you not understand, you savage?" he asked quietly. "Do you not know what protects me in this battle?"

The Skræling circled slightly, looking for superior tactical position.

"You are far too cautious to live. I have survived this fight because I do not care if I live or die!"

Mälar dove at the Skræling. His head smashed into the Skrælings's stomach. Both men flew backward. Mälar readied himself for the long twisting fall and a rapid, crushing death. He felt only joy.

The Eerhahkwoi shot out over the rapids and dropped like a stone. Mälar fell full-length onto the cliff edge, knocking the wind out of his lungs.

His head and arms hung over the ledge. Looking back over his shoulder, he saw that one foot had caught in the leggings of the choking Skræling, who lay on his side with his knees drawn up.

Mälar slid back onto the ledge. He pulled his foot free. He rolled over onto his back. He lay in a puddle of Skræling blood. Blood soaked his hair. Blood soaked what remained of his ragged tunic. Blood soaked his leggings. At his feet the Eerhahkwoi gagged and choked as he fought for the breath he would never draw.

Mälar looked at the ceiling of the cave.

He opened his mouth and laughed and laughed and laughed.

Labrans swung Mälar's sword in short arcs. The blade cut through the air, filling the thicket with deep whooshing sounds. He leapt at Usuthu, swinging the blade at Usuthu's face with all his new demonic strength. Usuthu sidestepped as quickly as the wind.

Mälar's sword buried itself into the earth. Usuthu slashed sideways with his curved blade, carefully measuring the strength of the blow. His sword severed the tendons at the back of Labrans' knee, but went no deeper.

Labrans toppled over onto that knee, but ignored the pain. He punched the Mongol in side with a short, stiff-armed blow. Grettir had given him great force. Usuthu felt as though he had been struck by the end of the ram used to smash down castle doors.

He back-stepped as his lungs seemed to collapse. Labrans retrieved his sword and took one hop toward the Mongol. He could not balance for a two-handed swing, but backed up the Mongol with rapid jabbing motions using the point of his blade.

Usuthu measured the distance. With one swift downward stroke he swept the fingers of Labrans' sword hand into the bushes. The sword dropped into the underbrush. Labrans raised a dagger in his other hand.

Usuthu dropped his sword and jumped at his brother's brother. He grabbed Labrans by the shoulders. Before the treacherous Northman could raise his knife, Usuthu butted him square in the forehead.

Labrans sat instantly. Stunned, he stared up at Usuthu. Blood dribbled from his fingerless hand. Blood leaked from the leg that would not move.

The dagger rested in open fingers that could not close. A trail of blood ran down his head.

Usuthu towered over him. Usuthu reached down, and carefully took Labrans' head in his huge hands. One hand rested over each of Labrans' ears.

"Do you want to know, Labrans," asked the Mongol in a calm, quiet voice, "why I've taken the care to kill you so thoroughly?"

Labrans could not reply.

"Your brother thought you enchanted," Usuthu continued, grinding his hands gently on Labrans' head. "He thought you were a victim of the witch's power. He thought you were a victim of his infidelity."

Usuthu began to squeeze the head between his hands.

"But," said the Mongol, "I know the truth."

He squeezed harder.

"I know you liked the power the witch offered you."

And harder.

"I know you stole an idol from the Skrælings on Vinland and worshiped it. I know that with your prayers to that idol you summoned Grettir."

Usuthu pushed hard on the skull. His tendons creaked from the effort and the veins in his arms swelled.

"I know," Usuthu shouted into the night, "that you betrayed your brother's trust and sought to kill him. You are no victim of witchcraft."

His voice rose to a shriek.

"You are its willing partner!"

Usuthu squeezed with all his might. Labrans'

head broke like an egg. The skull cracked and brains exploded into Usuthu's face. The Mongol squeezed until his hands touched. He smiled.

He happily rubbed his fingers together, balling brains and skull and hair into small, gooey mounds.

Halberd's hair hangs in his face in long sweaty ropes. His belly is slick with sweat. Ishlanawanda's back is drenched with it. Her mewing cries grow weaker and weaker as her voice leaves her. Still her slender hips drive back at Halberd. Still she reaches back to caress his thighs, to feel down below, as if to confirm that he is indeed her lover.

More times than he can count she has quickened her breathing to a scream and then collapsed in a series of small shudders. More times than he can count she has quickly roused herself and shoved her hips back at him once more.

Halberd can wait no longer.

"Ishlanawanda, my love, my sweet love."

"No," she murmurs, "wait."

With perfect dexterity she slowly flips over onto her back, sliding her legs open and then closed, never letting him slip outside her. Her face is covered with sweat. She opens her mouth to him and kisses him, raising her head and thrusting her tongue into his mouth again and again.

She holds his sweat-soaked hair in her hands and wraps her sweet, strong thighs around his waist.

"Now, my love," she whispers and moans. "Now, now now!"

The Voice of Love and Death

Halberd lies atop Ishlanawanda. He is spent, but still inside her. His head is burrowed into her shoulder and he licks her sweat. He glows with love and contentment. He knows that he is where he belongs. He feels her heart beat through her delicate rib cage.

Her back rests in the grass by the river. His knees rest on the ground. Birds sing over their heads. The river laps at its banks.

Ishlanawanda stiffens and gasps. Halberd raises his head and looks into her face. Her eyes are wide with fear. He looks over his shoulder.

Grettir floats above them.

Usuthu lay on the green floor of the thicket. Overhead, the sun broke through the night, filling the sky with light. At Usuthu's feet sat the headless carcass of Labrans.

Usuthu rubbed the bruise on his side. An odd noise made him look at the headless neck beside him. His blood froze and a chill shot down his back.

His bowels turned to ice water. For the only time in his life Usuthu felt fear while on dry land.

Grettir emerged from the bloody stump of Labrans' neck.

Mälar rested on the back of the Skræling who choked to death. He gazed at the Thundering Falls, watching it change color as the first rays of dawn struck its endless, green, curve.

He felt no need to hurry. Soon he would retrieve his ax and sword and pitch the bodies over the side. Then he would deal with his wounds and check Halberd's bandages. Shortly, he knew, Usuthu would return, bearing dinner. Or breakfast. Or midday meal.

A small cloud drifted out of the falls towards him. He straightened up for a better look. The cloud stopped just in front of the cliff edge. The blood left his face. He looked around for a sword but his arm would not move. He had sailed the world and seen much magic, but never anything to rival this.

Grettir hovered before him.

In a rasping seductive voice, a voice to bring chills to the neck of a corpse, a voice that might persuade a mother to slay her daughter, a voice of lust and murder, of sweetness and evil, of truest affection and eternal hatred: In the voice of love and death, Grettir spoke.

"Enjoy this moment while you may," she whispered, "Enjoy to its fullest. Sooner than you think, vengeance will be mine!"

In the vast intergalactic world of the future
the soldiers battle

NOT FOR GLORY

JOEL ROSENBERG

author of the bestselling
Guardian of the Flame series

Only once in the history of the Metzadan mercenary corps has a man been branded traitor. That man is Bar-El, the most cunning military mind in the universe. Now his nephew, Inspector-General Hanavi, must turn to him for help. What begins as one final mission is transformed into a series of campaigns that takes the Metzadans from world to world, into intrigues, dangers, and treacherous diplomatic games, where a strategist's highly irregular maneuvers and a master assassin's swift blade may prove the salvation of the planet—or its ultimate ruin . . .

There's an epidemic with 27 million victims. And no visible symptoms.

It's an epidemic of people who can't read.

Believe it or not, 27 million Americans are functionally illiterate, about one adult in five.

The solution to this problem is you... when you join the fight against illiteracy. So call the Coalition for Literacy at toll-free **1-800-228-8813** and volunteer.

Volunteer Against Illiteracy. The only degree you need is a degree of caring.